Faith in Rayne
Book 3 of the Rayne Saga

Dannie Marsden

Faith in Rayne
Book 3 of the Rayne Saga

Dannie Marsden

Affinity
Rainbow Publications

2017

Faith in Rayne
© 2017 by Dannie Marsden

Affinity E-Book Press NZ LTD
Canterbury, New Zealand

1st Edition

ISBN: 978-0-947528-51-5

This is a work of fiction. Names, character, places, and incidents are the product of the author's imagination or are used fictitiously and any resemblance to actual persons living or dead, businesses, companies, events, or locales is entirely coincidental

Editor: CK King
Proof Editor: Alexis Smith
Cover Design: Irish Dragon Designs

Acknowledgments

First I'd like to thank Annette Mori, for all being willing to give this story some of her focus. Annette, you saved me on this and I will forever be grateful. (PS check out her books at Affinity eBooks!!)

Deb, thank you for planting the idea to continue Rayne's story. Its fans like you that keep our vision alive.

Wendy, I thank you as well for the time you gave as well with this book. Please know that you are all special to me.

CK, for copy editing, and her help with making the book more authentic to the time period.

Last but most important, thanks to Julie, Mel, for supporting my work and Irish Dragon Designs for the fantastic cover. It is a privilege to work with all of you.

Dedication

I often joke that I'm a writer to keep the voices in my head from making me crazy. What I don't joke about is that it takes a special person to live with a writer as a spouse. Our spouses have to be willing to share us with, other men or women. They have to be willing to let us talk about our characters as if they are real, because at one point or another they are to us.

HJ, as always thank you for your support and encouragement. You will always be my dream woman come to life. You are my Lisbet.

Table of Contents

Also by Dannie Marsden

Luce Velazquez Learning to Live Again Series
Dress Blues
Desert Heat
Desert Blooms

Rayne Series

Rayne Comes to Town
Rayne's New Beginning

Single Stories

Thanksgivings
Affinity's Valentine Collection

Chapter One

The storm above was brewing, and it wouldn't be long before the clouds opened up and rain fell. The tired rider pulled the collar of the duster up to protect herself from the raindrops she knew would be pelting her any minute now. "Well, hell, I suppose this is to be expected given my damn luck lately," the rider muttered, as she spurred her horse into action. With all the trouble she felt nipping at her heels, she was overwhelmed with the need to put lifetimes between herself and the last town as quickly as possible. She couldn't be sure she was being followed, but she certainly didn't want to take a chance.

†

Rayne looked up at the sky and the dark, heavy clouds that hung low and threatened to drop their contents at any moment. "We need to get a move on, unless we want to be caught in the downpour that's headin' this way," she looked down at the blanket spread out in the grassy area in front of the creek. Her own smile grew wide when she spotted Ben and his enormous smile that was aimed at her. Never in a million years had she dreamt her life would have turned out this way. Lisbet was busy putting the remnants of the picnic away, while she spoke softly to the young child, whose complete attention was on Rayne.

"Come on, tiger, I don't reckon your ma wants to play your version of catch right now. Let me have that apple so I can give it to her, then you and I can take the basket back to the buckboard. What do you say?" Rayne knelt down beside the toddler and took the apple he offered. "Thank you, love, that's very good of you to hand that to me."

Standing to her full height again, she looked over at the woman who had begun making her life complete not too long ago. "Let me take the basket to the buckboard. I'll come back ta get the blanket and Ben, and we can head home. Hopin' we beat this storm. It looks like it's gonna be a hell of a downpour."

"Rayne, watch your language; Ben is picking up words left and right. Just the other day, I had to get on him for repeating your favorite word," Lisbet said, as she looked at Rayne. Her tone was serious, but the tenderness in her eyes showed her love, and it was clearly visible to anyone who knew them both.

"I'm sorry, I do need to pay closer attention to what I say. Be right back." She picked up the picnic basket and headed to the buckboard. With a happy heart, she couldn't help but smile at the thought that she now had someone in her life who paid attention to what and how she said things. She arranged the basket and headed back to the meadow and her small family. When Ben saw Rayne, he raised his arms, asking her to pick him up, which she did with complete joy. "Ok, tiger. Sweetheart, we ready to go?"

Lisbet glanced back at the spot where their blanket had just been spread out and sighed. The little, sad smile on her face told Rayne her sweetheart was disappointed and didn't want to leave. "Yes, hate leavin' this place, you know?"

"I know. But if we don't leave now, we're gonna get caught in whatever is in that nasty lookin' cloud," Rayne replied as they walked to the horses and the buckboard. "We'll come back soon, I promise."

The small family loaded up and was soon on their way back to their small ranch house. Ben fell asleep almost immediately, and the two women were left to enjoy each other's company and talk about the day they had just enjoyed and their plans for the rest of the evening.

Once life settled down for them, it didn't change much. For Rayne, there was always a fence to mend, a building to repair, and animals to feed. Lisbet dealt with meals, laundry, tending the home and Ben. Rayne couldn't be happier with the life they had. She felt truly blessed.

They were pulling into their homestead when the heavens opened up and giant drops of rain pelted down on them. Rayne pulled the wagon as close to the house as she could and jumped down. Taking Ben from Lisbet's arms, she carefully held the boy, as she helped her partner from the wagon. Once she had made sure her family was safely inside, she went back out and led the team of horses and the wagon to the barn.

Soon Rayne was in the barn, and with the big door closed to the elements she went about brushing down her horses. The horses were not only her work instruments, but were a much loved part of her life. The two palomino horses, Romeo and Juliette, were hard workers and she had pride in them. She spoke softly to Romeo as she brushed his coat. He would turn his head and nuzzle her just as soft while Juliette nibbled on her fresh grass, all while the wind howled and rain pelted the roof. Rayne had almost finished when the barn door slammed open with a blast of wind and rain. Rayne's head immediately went up, and her left hand dropped to the Colt strapped to her waist. The sudden movement stopped the stranger in an instant. "Whoa, I don't mean any harm. I'm just looking for some shelter," the woman held her hands up in the air.

"Sorry, I just wasn't expectin' anyone to be out in this weather. Come on in and unsaddle your horse. I got some fresh straw and oats over there. When you're done, we'll head to the house and get you warmed up and dried off. Looks to me like you're drenched."

"I am, thank you. I didn't mean to just barge in, and I hope you don't think I was aiming on stealing from you, because I wasn't."

"Well, thanks for tellin' me that. To be honest, if you were, you're outta luck. I ain't got two nickels to rub together." Rayne laughed, as she tried to put the stranger at ease. True, the woman had startled her, but her senses weren't screaming danger. She relaxed and hoped the stranger would as well. It wasn't long before the two were sufficiently at ease with each other and had finished brushing down the horses. "Well, looks like we're done." Rayne looked around at the settled horses. "Come on, let's head in. Lisbet should have supper on the table."

"No, I don't mean to impose. I was just looking for a dry place to spend the night," the stranger said. Rayne took a look at the unexpected guest, whose voice was most assuredly feminine and stood before her unmoving. If she had to guess, the female was about five foot four. She had brown hair and was a good looking woman.

"I ain't leavin' ya out here to starve." Rayne's tone didn't leave a whole lot of room to argue. "What's your name?" she asked.

"Oh, I'm sorry, I'm Eunice."

"Nice to meet ya, Eunice. I'm Rayne. Welcome to the Rockin M." Together the two headed to the main house. Rayne opened the door. "Lisbet, we got a visitor. You have enough grub to feed one more mouth?"

"Of course, don't be silly. We can always make room for more." Lisbet walked towards the two, wiping her hands dry. "Welcome, I'm Lisbet," she said to their guest. Lisbet extended her hand in welcome; her hooded eyes took in the stranger before landing on Rayne.

"Lisbet, this here is Eunice. Where's Ben?" Rayne asked, as she hung up her duster and hat.

"He's in his room playing with his toys."

"Thank you for your hospitality. I got caught in that storm and just needed some shelter and saw your barn. I didn't mean to cause any harm."

Eunice could only imagine how she looked to the blonde.

"Eunice, you have got to be gettin' chilled in those wet clothes. Come on, I'm sure I have somethin' that will fit you. Once you get dried, we can have supper. How does that sound?" Lisbet led the way to the bedroom. Her smile grew and spread a glow of warmth and welcome.

Rayne found herself alone in the sitting room with nothing to do. Questions raced through her mind about the stranger in their home. Who was Eunice, and what was she doing traveling alone? Didn't she realize that it wasn't safe for a single woman to ride the countryside without an escort? Hell, Rayne knew all too well, and she hadn't been dressed in women's clothing. Unwillingly, her mind went back to those months on the trail with the wagon train she'd joined. The single men made remarks about the women in the caravan behind their husband's backs, and Rayne saw the barely disguised, lustful looks they cast. She felt the rush of embarrassment creep up her neck, as she thought back on the few times she'd felt it was necessary for her to comment in order to keep her cover as a man.

Rayne heard the door to the bedroom open and close. She suspected this was to allow Eunice privacy to change and to give her and Lisbet a chance to talk.

"Where—" Lisbet abruptly stopped. "What's wrong sweetheart?" Lisbet quickly walked up to Rayne, who stood in front of the fire. Although it was spring, there was still a chill in the air at night.

"I was just rememberin' those days and nights on the trail. I wonder why she's travelin' alone. It ain't safe," Rayne said quietly, as her glance drifted to the closed bedroom door. She absently rubbed the back of her neck.

"That worries you doesn't it?" Lisbet wrapped her arms around Rayne's waist.

"Yeah, I know what men are like on the trail, the comments they make...scares me to think what could happen to her out there. What woulda happened to her if we weren't here?" Rayne asked.

"Have I told you lately just how much I love you?" Lisbet tilted her head up and brought Rayne's head down for a kiss.

Back in the bedroom, Eunice had finished changing out of the wet clothing and decided to take a look around the room. She took in the dark, cherry wood dresser, the hairbrushes that sat on top, and the wash bowl. Everything was simply beautiful, she thought, as her fingers brushed over the wood. She sighed as she wondered if she would ever make her house a home, with furnishings of her own. As her fingertips brushed across the polished wood, she thought about the two women who had taken her in. If you could go on appearances alone, these were good people, people she could truly like. What she felt most of all was love and acceptance, something she seldom found in her travels. She would give anything to feel that in her hometown. Friends, she wished she had friends. She shook off the loneliness and walked to the door.

Rayne and Lisbet were in each other's arms kissing when Eunice took a couple of steps into the parlor. When she saw the two women, she was both embarrassed at what she saw and intrigued. She knew from her time as a prostitute that some women enjoyed other women. She herself had never engaged in that sort of relationship. Standing there watching the two women share an intimate moment, she felt a little curious. Eunice carefully backed into the bedroom, where she took a moment to compose herself. She spoke loudly as she re-entered the sitting room. "I can't begin to tell you how wonderful dry clothes feel."

Lisbet took a step back and turned to Eunice. "I can imagine. I'm so glad we are able to help you. Storms this time of year can be terrible. Where are you headed to?"

"Colorado, I'm meeting up with my husband and his cousin." Eunice saw a look pass between Rayne and Lisbet and wondered what it was all about. Feeling the subtle shift in the mood between the two, Eunice felt she had inadvertently brought up something she shouldn't have, but she had no idea what.

"I see." Lisbet brushed at her apron. "Supper's waitin'. Rayne, show our guest to the table while I get Ben."

"I'm sorry, I didn't mean to upset Lisbet," Eunice said, as Lisbet walked away.

"She'll be fine," Rayne replied, as she led the way to the table.

"Are you sure?" Eunice was not convinced that she hadn't just given a reason to be put out in the cold rain.

"Yeah, ain't nothin' we won't work through," Rayne said. "I hope you don't mind venison stew."

Lisbet walked towards the table with Ben toddling beside her. "Will you look at him, who is this handsome young man?" Eunice asked, as she watched the toddler walk with Lisbet's help.

"This is Ben, our son." Rayne's smile was huge, as she lifted the boy and playfully tossed him up in the air. Ben immediately began giggling.

A few months prior, Rayne had brought up her plans for the Rockin' M Ranch; they involved expanding.

The expansion itself wasn't what bothered the blonde. Colorado was the issue. In Lisbet's mind, Colorado was filled with danger. She imagined murderers and thieves just waiting for an unsuspecting person to walk by to rob, and women were most definitely not safe. The mines were teeming with men who had not seen a woman in who knows how long and were ready to assault any female that happened by. It scared her that Rayne couldn't see that. The couple began having heated discussions about this expansion. Each argument left Lisbet feeling like she was keeping Rayne from a dream, as though she was keeping Rayne trapped. That was the last thing she ever wanted. To say that the point had become a sore spot in their relationship would be putting it mildly.

At the mention of Colorado, Lisbet's heart sank. She knew they would be discussing the topic, and once again, they would disagree.

Lisbet did her best to put her thoughts aside and focus on what was happening around her dinner table. "Rayne, don't get him goin'. We'll never get him to calm down enough to eat, let alone go to bed," Lisbet admonished. She couldn't help but smile; she loved seeing Rayne play with Ben. During the last two and a half years, Rayne had become a different woman. When they met, Rayne was lonely and lost. Although she'd allowed a complete stranger into her home and into her life, she remained guarded. After everything with her father settled and they let go of the fear of losing Ben, Rayne began to laugh more. She'd opened up in a way Lisbet had never expected.

"Okay, tiger, Momma says that we have to calm down some. So what do you say we sit right here and have some dinner?" Rayne smiled at Ben. "Hey, say hello to Eunice. She's our new friend."

Ben buried a shy smile in Rayne's shoulder, his pudgy little finger in his mouth.

"Hello, sweetie," Eunice said softly.

Ben pulled his head away from the shoulder; his blue eyes sparkled, as he smiled and looked at Eunice. With his wet finger, he reached out and touched Eunice's cheek and quietly said, "Lo."

With a laugh, Eunice said, "What a sweetheart."

"Yes, he is at the moment; but trust me, he is a handful the rest of the time." Lisbet's smile showed the pride and love she felt towards her family.

"Ain't that the truth." Rayne placed the boy in his high chair. "Come on sit, the stew's gettin' cold." She nodded at a chair and took her seat.

Eunice looked around at the family who had opened their door to her and, for a moment, felt a pang of regret. A part of her ached at the fact that she didn't have children; but given how her life had turned out, it was probably for the best that the good Lord hadn't seen fit to allow her any so far. Maybe when she settled in Telluride.

Lisbet dished up bowls of the stew, slices of bread, and glasses of cool water. Rayne offered a prayer of thanks for the food, their safety, and new friends. When she finished, they raised their heads and began to eat.

"So, Eunice, you said a little bit ago that you're headin' to Colorado to meet up with your husband. Mind if I ask what he does for a livin'?" Rayne asked.

"Harry is going to mine silver and gold. He won the claim to a mine there in Telluride, so he and Robert are heading there soon to set up their operation." Eunice looked at her bowl, then at Ben, but she wouldn't meet Rayne or Lisbet's eyes.

What am I doing? These people opened up their home to me, and here I am lying to them.

"Rayne, I don't think you should pry into Eunice's business. If she wants to tell us she will." Lisbet's tone was sharp.

"Lisbet, I was just makin' conversation is all."

"Oh no, please, she isn't prying at all," Eunice said quickly.

"Where are you originally from?" Rayne asked.

Eunice chuckled at the look she saw Lisbet flash Rayne. She remembered that look fondly from her childhood. It was the one her mother would give her when she was getting out of hand. She even gave something akin to that look to Harry from time to time.

"San Antonio actually, that's where I met Harry," Eunice replied.

"Lots of cattle out that way." Rayne nodded.

"Yes, there are. Harry had actually thought of starting a cattle ranch at one time."

"Oh? I take it by the fact that he is starting a mining operation that he didn't, how come?" Rayne asked.

"Oh, he just found something that caught his interest more, I suppose," Eunice said.

She thought about the real reason his cattle ranch never came to fruition. Mentally shaking herself from her thoughts, Eunice smiled. "This stew is so good. I can't tell you how much I appreciate your hospitality. I was looking at a dark barn, a biscuit, and some jerky otherwise."

Lisbet gave a half smile and mumbled a thank you. Rayne reached over and wiped Ben's mouth. "Okay pal, you're done. You've started playin' so come on, let's get you cleaned up and get you calmed down for bed. What do ya say?"

"Tory mama. Tory peas." Ben reached his chubby arms to Rayne.

"Well of course, I'll read you a story. But let's clean up first." Rayne lifted up her son. "Sorry, when he gets like this it's impossible to get him back to eating," she apologized to the guest.

"It's not a problem, really, I taught school for a while, so I know how kids can be," Eunice smiled at the boy in Rayne's arms.

"You're a teacher?" Lisbet asked.

"Yes, I was. Then I met Harry, and well, he didn't want me to continue, so I resigned and then he decided to go and get itchy feet and…well, here I am on my way out west."

"Do you miss it?" she asked.

"Sometimes, I do. You get used to having little kids around, hearing their voices, the way they talk, the way they just accept people for how they are with no judgment." She tried to stay in the present and not go to the place where she heard snippets of comments made about her or saw people turn to avoid her or speak behind their hands.

Lisbet couldn't help but notice how Eunice withdrew and the look in her eyes that Lisbet clearly remembered from her own childhood. She wondered what it was that Eunice was remembering, what it was that she was running from. *It doesn't matter, who am I to judge?* She knew the world was a cruel place if you didn't behave or live a certain way. Take for example her and Rayne, she knew in the eyes of some people their love was wrong and they should be run out of town or hung from the nearest tree. She simply nodded.

"Yes, they do. I know our lives were completely changed the moment Ben came to us."

"Please, don't think I'm prying, but it's obvious you and Rayne aren't sisters... Do you mind if I ask..." Eunice paused, not sure how to ask what she already suspected.

"Rayne and I live our life as a married couple. I'm hopin' that doesn't change your opinion of us," Lisbet said in a defensive manner.

"It isn't up to me to judge how others live their lives," Eunice replied. "You said when Ben came into your lives... Ben isn't Rayne's son?"

"We are raisin' him as ours, but he is her nephew. He was six months old when he came to live with us. It's a long story. When the family showed up here, Ben's mother had passed away, and his father wasn't far behind. Jason died about twelve hours after he showed up," Lisbet said, as she went about gathering their dishes.

"And he is what, about three years old?"

"Yes, feels like he's always been a part of our lives. Rayne adores him, and he obviously adores her." Lisbet smiled.

"And they both adore you," Eunice commented, as she stood and started to help clean up. "How long have you and Rayne been... No, don't answer that, I shouldn't pry," Eunice quickly said, as she saw Lisbet pause for a split second.

"You aren't. Rayne and I don't hide what we are, least not in our home, but we don't flaunt it either. So when someone asks out of the blue like that, I'm caught by surprise. We've been together about three years. Most folks in town know about us, and help keep our secret with those that don't."

Eunice smiled as she thought about her time with Harry. Then the smile slowly faded. She loved him, and while she was happy with life, she sometimes just wished for a little more. What was wrong with wanting a home in one place? Not always feeling the need to explore different places and always running off. Just once, she would like to feel that Harry was happy just being with her.

"Are you all right?" Lisbet asked.

"Yeah, I'm just tired. Long few days, you know?"

"I'm sorry, I should have thought about that. Sit, you don't have to help. Go sit by the fire and relax. I'll bring you some coffee."

Eunice nodded and smiled, then walked to the living area and sat on the sofa. Eunice could hear Rayne in the background as she told a story to Ben. As she listened, her eyes closed. It wasn't long before she was asleep.

Chapter Two

Lisbet stood at the kitchen window, watching Rayne pace back and forth along the fenced corral, stop and stare out over the prairie, then pace some more. In the week since Eunice appeared at their barn, Lisbet had watched Rayne grow increasingly fidgety. With a soft sigh, she pushed away from the sink and walked out the door to where Rayne stood.

"What are you thinkin' about, sweetheart?" Lisbet asked, as she approached Rayne, who was staring out over the prairie.

"Nothin' really. Where's Eunice?" Rayne replied.

"She's playin' with Ben. I'm amazed at how quickly he took a likin' to her. I'm worried at how he's gonna handle it when she finally leaves." Lisbet leaned against the fence and cocked her head to the side, looking at her spouse.

"Oh, I'm sure he'll be fine. He's resilient ya know." Rayne's eyes still focused on the prairie. She sighed. "These damned storms need to stop; they're makin' the plantin' down right miserable."

"It ain't the rain that's buggin' you. So, why don't you just get it off your chest?" Lisbet folded her arms.

"I think it's time to expand. We've talked about it before, what do you think?"

"Depends on where you want to expand to. I think expandin' around here is a good idea, and I ain't got a problem with that. What I ain't wild about is expandin' out west."

"It ain't like I'm crazy about the idea of leavin' you and Ben for any length of time. Ya know that. But dammit, Lisbet, from all I hear, Colorado is filled with prime cattle land just ripe for the takin'."

"You ain't gonna let this go, are ya?" Lisbet turned and looked out at the open prairie that held Rayne's gaze.

Rayne turned to the shorter woman who stood beside her. She saw the pain in her eyes and could hear it in her voice. She looked away again. "Lisbet, you know how much land is goin' for around these parts, and it ain't even prime. If we're gonna expand, it makes sense to make sure that whatever land we buy is damned good and will be able to handle the herds we put on it. From what I'm hearin', land there in Colorado is cheap. Hun, I mean, it's worth a look, don't ya think?" Rayne spoke softly, as she once again turned her gaze to the blonde woman who had captured her heart when she didn't realize she still had a heart to be captured.

Tears glistened in Lisbet's eyes. "When you thinkin' of leavin', and how long you plannin' on bein' gone?"

"I ain't sure. I suppose the sooner I can get goin' the sooner I can get things started there. I'll be needin' to talk with Tom and Mark, get somethin' set up so's the operation here keeps goin' and you ain't got nothing added to your chores. The ranch is doin' good right now, and John is more than capable of seein' to the day to day matters. I think things here will be fine. My main concern is you and Ben."

Lisbet wiped a tear away. "I don't see how runnin' to someplace in Colorado shows that concern right now." She pushed away from the fence and briskly walked away.

"Wait," Rayne called out. Lisbet didn't stop, and Rayne simply watched her walk back to the house.

Eunice looked up from her spot on the floor, where she had been playing with Ben and his blocks, to see Lisbet wiping tears from her eyes as she briskly walked to the bedroom and closed the door. Eunice quietly said to Ben, who looked up at his momma as she closed the door, "Why don't you stay right here while I check on your momma, hmm? How about you build a nice big castle okay? I'll be right back, sweetheart." Eunice stood up, walked to the closed door, and gently knocked.

"Yes?"

"Lisbet, is everything okay?" she asked, as she opened the door.

"Eunice, I really don't want to talk about it right now, but thank you for checkin' on me." Lisbet wiped her eyes.

"I know you don't know me well, but I'm a good listener and...well, I feel...both you and Rayne have opened your home to me, and I want to return your kindness."

"I'm sorry Eunice, it's...I just don't know what to do. Rayne wants to head to Colorado and expand. I don't know what Colorado is like, what dangers are there, oh God... I can't imagine life without her," Lisbet said from the bed where she sat.

"I understand why you would be afraid, and I doubt there is anything I can say that would change your mind. The truth is Colorado is untamed, it's wild. Crikey, it's the west, but someday it will be civilized. The few that help tame it can, I'd imagine, have a fortune at their feet. Do you really want to keep Rayne from that?" Eunice leaned against the door she had just walked through.

"I don't, but why can't she have that here? This ranch is doin' just fine, we got a nice sized herd, and we're gettin' by just fine."

"I understand you feel that way, but I'm not so sure Rayne does." Eunice pushed away from the door and turned the doorknob. There really wasn't anything else she could say. If Lisbet wanted to talk about it more, she would. In silence, Eunice walked back to the sitting room where Ben sat playing with his toys.

It was almost thirty minutes later that Rayne opened the door. Eunice looked up at the entrance and smiled as Rayne stepped in. Rayne hung up her hat, looked over at the two and beamed when Ben turned in her direction. She walked over to him and kneeled down beside him. "Hey there, tiger, what are ya buildin'? Oh! Would ya look at that, ain't it a beauty?" Rayne nodded towards the closed door. "She in the bedroom?"

"Yes, she is, and she's really upset."

"Yup, I know." Rayne stood up with a sigh. She walked to the door and gently tapped before entering.

Rayne closed the door behind her and leaned against it. "Lisbet, I don't know what you want me to say."

"I want you to say that you'll stay here and forget this fool idea of expandin' into Colorado. I want you to say that you're happy with everythin' we have here, with our life here." Lisbet wiped away a tear as it fell.

Rayne walked farther into the room with her hands in her pockets. "Lisbet, of course I love our life and everythin' in it. Is it so wrong to want absolutely everythin' for my family? That I don't want you or Ben to have to ever worry about money? I'm sorry, but I don't think it is."

"No, of course not. I just don't know why you have to do that from some godforsaken place in Colorado." Lisbet twisted the hankie she held in her hands.

Rayne pinched the bridge of her nose. "At one time this place was considered godforsaken. Look at it now. California was the same way, and Colorado will follow suit. I think the Rockin M should be part of its history. Lisbet, I want Ben to be a doctor or a lawyer...oh hell, the president even. Somethin' other than a rancher or a farmer. Somethin' he ain't gonna be breakin' his back at just to make ends meet. That means a good education; and that means college, which is expensive." Rayne leaned against the dresser, her eyes on the green-eyed blonde who sat on the bed.

With a snort Lisbet replied, "I'm well aware that colleges are expensive, and of course, I want the same things for him. I just don't happen to agree with where you think you have to be to earn that money. Look, I realize you've already made the decision to go and nothin' I say is gonna change your mind. Just give me that I have, at least, the right to be upset."

"Of course you got that right, hun. Just trust that I won't do anythin' to put my life in jeopardy. Sweetheart, I got too much to come back to." Rayne pushed herself off the dresser and walked to Lisbet. "I waited too long to have all

19

this, you, Ben. I ain't gonna throw it away," she finished as she knelt in front of the smaller woman.

"It ain't about trust Rayne. It's about you goin' off to a place that's wild and filled with people who don't understand people like you and me, a place filled with Lord only knows what. You better come back to us. You hear me?"

"Always," Rayne whispered softly.

Lisbet cleared her throat and wiped at her eyes. "I suppose I should get supper on the table. You'll be wantin' to see to the horses."

Rayne gave a slight nod and stood. "Yup, unless it rains again tonight, I'm hopin' to get some plantin' done tomorrow. So, they'll need their strength. Lisbet…"

"I know, we'll be fine," the smaller woman finished Rayne's sentence and walked to the door of the bedroom, opened it, and walked out.

Supper that evening was a quiet affair. Although Rayne tried to engage in conversation with Lisbet and lighten the mood, Lisbet wasn't having any of it. Answers were kept to a bare minimum. Once everyone was done, she was up and clearing away the dishes and washing them.

†

Eunice played with Ben and kept him occupied, while Rayne sat at her desk going over ledgers and scribbling out plans for her upcoming trip.

It was hours later that Rayne looked up with blurred eyes and realized she was alone. With the house quiet, she closed her eyes. Never had she dreamt she could be so happy. She had everything she'd ever hoped for. Someone she loved with all her heart and a happy and healthy toddler running around. She had a thriving ranch and good friends who were always there to lend a hand when needed. Was it a mistake to hope for the same in a different place?

Maybe Lisbet was right; maybe she was gambling it all away. No, her heart told her she was making the right move. With a sigh, she whispered to herself, "No one ever said life was easy." She closed her ledgers and tucked away her notes, then reached for the lantern and turned the light down before standing and stretching. She made sure the fire had enough wood to keep them warm through the slight chill of the early morning hours and headed for the bedroom.

†

Rayne slipped into bed quietly. She pulled the blankets over herself and Lisbet, leaning close to gently place a kiss on the creamy shoulder, even as her hand moved to the soft curve of Lisbet's hip. Her lips dropped more tender kisses along the soft shoulder and neck.

Lisbet rolled over, her hands moving to the woman's shoulders. "Rayne—" she whispered and caught her bottom lip between her teeth. Her eyes locked with Rayne's, and a sigh escaped her lips as a tear fell from the corner of her eye.

Rayne reached over and gently wiped the tear away. "Maybe you're right. Maybe I'm bein' foolish; my place is here with you and Ben. We have a good life, the ranch thrives. I don't need to be runnin' off anywhere."

With a growl, Lisbet responded, "God, Rayne. Don't do this. If you wanna go, go, but don't look to me to make that decision for you. *No*, I don't want you to go for Lord knows how long, but I'm not gonna make you stay either. I

21

will, however, be here waitin' for you to come get us. So you better hurry up and make all these plans happen." Lisbet pulled Rayne's head down towards hers and claimed the warm lips.

"I'll do my best," Rayne whispered.

"Shut up and make love to me."

"With pleasure," Rayne replied breathlessly before she claimed the sweet lips again. It was hours later before they finally fell asleep in each other's arms.

†

It was the growing, warm rays of the sun shining into the room that woke Rayne. Well, the smell of coffee drifting in from the kitchen helped. She looked over and saw Lisbet slowly waking. With a smile, she whispered, "Good mornin', darlin'."

Lisbet smiled as she opened her eyes. "Mm, good mornin'."

The sound of Ben playing in the next room reached her ears. "Oh Lord, I need to get up. Ben is already awake."

"Eunice has him. I know she has coffee goin', I can smell it brewin'. Hey where ya goin'?" Rayne reached out to grab Lisbet.

"Eunice is up, she has coffee goin', and Ben is up. I'm sure she has to be thinkin' I'm loungin' away back here ignorin' my chores and home." Lisbet quickly threw on her dress.

"I highly doubt she is thinkin' you're loungin' around."

"Rayne Mathews, Oh Lord, you don't think she..." Lisbet shrieked, horrified.

"I just meant, she probably just thinks we overslept. And even if she did think about it, so what, it's our home. Hell, she's probably thinkin' that I'm one damned lucky woman." Rayne had a big smile on her face. "And I certainly am one hell of a lucky woman. Last night was amazin'."

Lisbet stopped at the door, glanced over her shoulder, and flashed a smile of her own. "Mm yes, it was. And now I need to get breakfast goin'."

Breakfast, for Rayne, consisted of a steaming cup of coffee and a biscuit with some canned preserves. With the decision made to head west, she wanted to make sure things at the Rockin' M were set to run smoothly for Lisbet and her ranch hand. That meant the remaining ground needed to be worked up and crops in the ground. She wanted to ride the fences and make sure they were sturdy, make sure the cattle were healthy. With a smile on her face and whistling a tune, she headed out the door.

Eunice looked up from the picture book she was looking at with Ben. "Lisbet, why don't you pack a picnic lunch, take some nice, cold lemonade, and have a quiet meal with Rayne?"

"Oh, Eunice, I couldn't possibly do that."

"Why not?"

"Cuz of all the things that need to be done around here. There's laundry to do, a house that needs to be kept, not to mention the garden and chickens and Ben. I can't just expect you to watch him."

†

Rayne took her hat off and wiped the sweat from her forehead. She looked to the vibrant blue sky with scattered puffy, white clouds and a bright yellow sun that put off rays of heat. The scent of freshly turned soil and warm grass was in her nose, and with a satisfied sigh, she reached for her canteen. She was taking a long drink, when she spotted a rider heading towards her. Soft and low, she spoke to her horse. "Yup, I see em'."

Romeo snorted and brought his front hoof down on the ground as his head bobbed, as if to say he understood the words his master had uttered.

The rider came closer into view, and Rayne realized it was Lisbet. Her heart skipped a beat.

"It's Lisbet, and since she doesn't seem to be in a hurry, you can calm down."

Rayne slipped the canteen over her head and shoulder, swung it to her back, and put the black Stetson back on her head. She walked to the front of the big palomino and stroked his velvet-soft nose. "Maybe we can take a rest, would you like that boy? I know I could sure use one. You stay put while I go see what's goin' on. Ya hear?" she spoke to the big horse, as she unhitched the plow.

Rayne walked towards the approaching rider, her smile growing bigger as she spotted the picnic basket. "What brings you out here, darlin'?" she asked as the painted horse came to a stop.

"Well, Eunice thought you might like a nice cold glass of lemonade, some lunch maybe. I hope you don't mind...I...she offered to keep Ben, and I thought..." Lisbet trailed off. "You're not upset are you?"

"She offered?"

"Well of course she did, I wouldn't have dreamt of imposin' by asking her. I've never up and left Ben, and I'd never do somethin' this impulsive, I just..."

"Darlin' that's my point. Now, just calm down and give me a kiss."

As soon as their lips touched, Lisbet relaxed and melted in towards the solid form that was Rayne. The kiss that was meant to welcome and reassure Lisbet quickly became hungry, and Rayne dropped the picnic basket to embrace the smaller woman tightly.

Lisbet playfully pushed at Rayne's shoulders and breathlessly pulled away from the kiss. "What about lunch? You must be starvin'."

"Oh I am but not for what you have in that there basket. I aim to finish what we started last night," Rayne's voice was husky.

"But my love, we did finish. And to my recollection, more than once."

"Woman, just the sight of you sets my blood on fire, and I swear to God, there is nothin' in this world that quenches that thirst. Now where's that picnic blanket? I don't want you lyin' on rocks while I enjoy your body again."

The simple declaration brought a rush of warmth to Lisbet's face and a small flame of desire in her lower body. "It's in the basket, on top." Her heart leaped with joy. *This amazin', beautiful, strong woman wants me, still. Dear Lord, how did I get so lucky?*

Rayne let go and reached for the basket and the reins of the horse that was busy eating grass, then led them all towards a grouping of trees. Once she reached a spot with shade, she tethered Romeo, who happily found a another patch of grass to graze on. While she reached for the blanket, she whistled for Apache, who lifted his head and slowly walked towards the group. Lisbet reached an end of the blanket, and together they spread it out. Apache joined the other horse and, with a snort, began to graze on the grass as well. Lisbet smiled. "You think you have us all trained, don't you?"

"Yup, it's a gift." Rayne had a big smile on her face, as she took her hat off and tossed it towards the blanket. She crooked her finger and beckoned. "Now come here."

Lisbet's breath hitched even as she obeyed.

Rayne's eyes darkened, and as she watched Lisbet draw close, she reached out and tenderly brushed back the long hair. She dropped her head to kiss the soft, waiting lips. The kiss was tender, and Rayne gently sucked on Lisbet's bottom lip. One hand supported the blonde's lower back, drawing her closer; the fingers of Rayne's other hand wrapped in the blonde locks.

Lisbet moaned into Rayne's mouth, as Rayne tugged at lips with her teeth. "God, all I've thought about this mornin' has been you," Rayne whispered as she pulled away. Her hands moved to the front of Lisbet's dress, to the small buttons that held it closed. Her fingers deftly undid each button before parting the material, as her mouth found its way to the column of Lisbet's neck and the visible pulse point.

Lisbet inhaled sharply as Rayne kissed her neck, and Lisbet's fingers tugged at the shirt Rayne wore, pulling it from the waistband of the trousers that hugged her hips.

Rayne's lips left a trail of kisses along the soft skin of Lisbet's neck down to the gentle curve of her collar bone, as she pushed the material of the dress off the creamy shoulders and let it fall to the ground. Rayne took a moment to let her own shirt drop, before she helped the blonde down to the blanket. She settled herself next to her and continued placing kisses on the sweet lips, as her hands and fingers moved over the woman's body. Slowly, the kisses moved down the slender neck to the swell of Lisbet's breast before stopping at the dark, hard peak of her nipple.

Rayne's tongue flicked over the hard nub, before she sucked it into her mouth, her heartbeat increasing by the second. Rayne felt Lisbet's fingers clutching at her hair, and as she pulled back, she reached for the hand, pulled it away from her hair, and returned her attention to the hard nipple.

Lisbet moaned softly, as her hand moved to Rayne's solid shoulders hovering over her.

Rayne once again, pulled back and reached for Lisbet's arms. With both hands, she pushed them above Lisbet's head. "Keep them right there, ya hear me?" she said with a wicked smile.

A gasp escaped Lisbet's lips.

Rayne returned her attention and her lips to the woman's body. With her weight supported on one elbow, she dropped kisses even as her hand roamed.

Lisbet's hands, once again, started roaming, reaching for Rayne's shoulders and hair as she attempted to pull them closer together.

Rayne growled, as she lifted her head and grabbed the hands. "I said, keep 'em there. Move 'em again and we start all over."

Lisbet groaned. "But I want to touch you. Please, Rayne."

"No," Rayne replied.

Rayne knew the look in her eyes and the light touch of her fingers moving over Lisbet's stomach to the delicate blonde curls of her womanhood had lit the flame of desire that would pool between Lisbet's thighs.

Rayne slowly inched her way over the path her fingers had just trailed, dropping kisses. Her fingertips moved between the creamy thighs and felt the heat and moisture coming from Lisbet's center. With a groan of pleasure, she allowed her fingers to glide over the opening and over the hard nub of Lisbet's clit.

Lisbet arched up, her eyes dazed. "Rayne, please, I need to touch you."

"No, you keep your hands put," Rayne commanded. She nipped gently at the flesh of Lisbet's inner thigh, before her tongue flicked closer to the silky nectar of Lisbet's desire.

"God, you taste so good," she said, as she positioned herself between her love's legs. With her tongue licking and flicking over the nub, she drove Lisbet towards the edges of pleasure. With each flick of her tongue, Lisbet's heartbeat pounded harder in the vein of her neck, and Rayne could hear her breath strain in a collection of moans and groans, throaty and husky.

Rayne felt the orgasm building in Lisbet with each stroke of her fingers and flick of her tongue. She felt the trembling and quivering overtake Lisbet and felt herself join the woman she loved more than life in heaven. The two laid contentedly in each other's arms, enjoying the warmth of the sun on their bodies and the fresh scent of the wildflowers in the air.

After a while, Lisbet reached for her dress, as Rayne stretched out on the blanket with a satisfied smile. "What are you smilin' at?" Lisbet asked, a knowing smile on her own lips.

"Oh, I was just thinkin' that you have the look of a well-loved woman on your face."

"Well, maybe that's because I am," Lisbet replied softly.

"That's good, but why'd you get dressed already? Maybe I wasn't done lovin' ya yet."

"Lord, you are in a mood, aren't you?" Lisbet blushed. She reached for Rayne's shirt and tossed it to her lovingly. "Get yourself dressed and eat somethin'. The day's wastin', and you still got some work to do." She got some chicken out of the basket, along with cheese and biscuits.

"I suppose, but somehow I'm thinkin' that there chicken and work ain't as good as what we just shared. I cain't imagine anything as delicious as that." Rayne stood as she buttoned her shirt to tuck it into her pants.

"Yes, well, I don't see how that will help get the crops planted. And besides, I'll need to get back. I can't leave Eunice to watch Ben all day."

"If she knew what you been up to, I doubt she would mind all that much," Rayne snickered.

"Oh my Lord. Will you stop? I swear you say things like that just to get a rise outta me," Lisbet replied in mock irritation.

"Maybe. I do love that little rush of color that hits your face. But you're right; this field ain't gonna get planted if I don't finish plowin'. How about I quit early though, and we hitch up the wagon and head into town? Stop in and see Mark and Tom, maybe have a supper at Bessie's. What do you say?"

Lisbet smiled big. "That sounds like a fine idea. I'll let Eunice know, and she can join us! It'll be fun to introduce her to our friends before you and her take off. I assume that's what you'll want to talk to Mark and Tom about." Lisbet's mood changed slightly. Rayne had made the decision, and she would not be the reason Rayne didn't follow her dream.

Chapter Three

Lisbet rode to the homestead with a smile on her lips and love in her heart. She had just spent a good portion of the day with the woman she loved. Now she had an impromptu evening with friends planned, both old and new. She couldn't wait to introduce their new friend, Eunice, to Tom, Sally, Mark, Emily, and Bessie. She hoped they would adore her.

Her smile turned into disappointment when Eunice declined the invitation. She said she didn't want to go into town and what was the point of meeting people she would never see again.

"What do you mean, you won't be seeing them again? Don't you plan on visiting Rayne and me?"

"Well, I'm hoping that when I visit you and Rayne and Ben, it will be because you're all living in Telluride. To be honest, I'm really not much of a traveler."

"But you would really like Tom and Sally. And I know Emily and Bessie would simply adore you," Lisbet countered.

"You and Rayne enjoy yourselves. I'll be content right here. In fact, I could use a little alone time with just my thoughts," Eunice said with a smile. *Please just leave it alone. I just can't take the risk of someone recognizing me.*

"Are you sure? I feel horrible leavin' you here."

"I'm positive. I will enjoy an evening alone. In fact, I might just read one of those dime novels I see sitting on the shelf over there." Eunice walked towards the few books that were propped up on a shelf. "I've always wanted to read about Butch Cassidy and his partner. Stories I hear are wild. I wonder if they are true," she said, as she ran a finger over the spine of one of the books.

"Oh, from what Rayne and Tom say, those two are bad ones. Tom says the books don't even tell half the story," Lisbet replied with excitement.

"Oh really? How does Tom know about them, I mean, other than what is in these books?" Eunice asked with interest.

"Tom is the sheriff in Willow Springs; he has wanted posters of them. There's even talk about there bein' a woman that travels with them."

"Are there any posters of her?"

"Not that I know of. Rayne would probably know more about that than I do. Are you sure you don't want to go with us?"

"I'm positive, but thank you for the offer."

†

Rayne rode up to the corral and jumped off her horse. She took the saddle off and brushed him down, then gave him a bucket of oats. "There ya go boy, ya done a good job today. I gotta go get cleaned up! Got a date in town with a beautiful woman and a handsome little man." With a spring in her step, she headed for the house.

"Hey there, got some bathwater for me?" she asked, as she stepped into the house. "What's goin' on?" she asked when she spotted the women.

"Nothin' really, I was just tryin' to convince Eunice to join us this evenin'. She doesn't want to, says she would much rather stay here and read those dime novels you have about Butch Cassidy and Sundance." Lisbet ran her hands down the sides of her skirt. "There's some water heating up for you, let me check on it."

"You sure you don't want to go with us?" Rayne asked.

"Yes, I'm sure. I'll be fine, I promise you."

"Interested in Butch Cassidy, are ya? From what I hear, for an outlaw, he's a decent fella. I mean as decent as ya can be and steal from good folks."

"Do you think maybe those stories really are true? I can't believe that he is as bad as they say." Eunice brought her hand up to her head and smoothed back her hair that was already in a neat bun.

"Well, I suppose it cain't all be true, but I also cain't see so many people lyin' about him. Suppose the one good thing about him is he makes it a point to never kill anyone. Look, I need to go get cleaned up. You sure you don't wanna come with us? I know everyone would love to meet ya."

"Yes, but thank you for thinking of me." Eunice turned, once again looking at the dime novel.

"Bathwater is ready," Lisbet said, as she came into the room. "And Ben just woke up from his nap."

"Sounds good, I cain't tell you how nice a hot bath sounds," Rayne said. Before turning towards the bedroom and the cast iron tub that sat in the corner, she walked to the shelf Eunice stood in front of and pulled out a book. "This one here is a fairly new one. I think you'd much rather read about Annie Oakley. Accordin' to that there book, she and Buffalo Bill are havin' a grand old time with that Wild West show they got goin' on." Rayne smiled while she handed the book to Eunice and walked towards the bath Lisbet had drawn for her.

Eunice stared at the woman posing with a rifle on the cover of the book she'd just been handed. She stifled annoyance that brewed in her blood and feigned interest in the book. She could feel Lisbet's eyes on her. She smiled as she looked at the blonde. "Well, it does look like it's interesting. I think I shall thoroughly enjoy reading this."

"Rayne is right, I found it fascinatin'. Can you imagine all the places they've been? Anyway, I do wish you were goin' with us instead of stayin' here. But I can understand wantin' a little bit of time alone. With Ben around, it does get quite loud at times, and with Rayne walkin' in and out. I'm sorry, here I am tellin' ya how noisy it can be, and all you're wantin' is some quiet. You know where everything is, so please, make yourself at home."

"Thank you, Lisbet. I do hope that you enjoy your evening out."

"I'm sure we will, thank you. I'll make sure we don't make too much noise when we come back. I know you'll be sleepin'. Oh, there's Rayne callin' me," Lisbet replied.

As Lisbet went to see what Rayne wanted, Ben walked up to Eunice and gave her a big smile. He had his little index finger in his mouth, and his blue eyes just sparkled. It was hard to imagine his smile getting any brighter, but it did when Eunice smiled back at him. Eunice had to admit, if only to herself, the little boy melted her heart and made her wish even harder that she had one of her own. She knelt down and asked, "Are you ready for your trip to town?"

"I go Uncle Tom!" Ben said excitedly.

"That sounds like fun."

"You go?" Ben asked in a shy voice.

"Oh…no honey, I'm going to stay here and do some reading, enjoy some alone time."

Lisbet walked back into the parlor with her bonnet in her hand. "Ben, leave Eunice alone now. Come on, Ma's about ready to go." She reached for his little jacket. She was quickly followed by Rayne, who once more asked if Eunice was sure she didn't want to join them. When Eunice declined, the small family walked outside to the horse and wagon that waited for them.

Chapter Four

Tom Kennedy was walking the boarded sidewalks, when he spotted the wagon coming up the street. He squinted and smiled, as the wagon drew closer. With a happy shake of his head, he stepped into the doorway of the small diner and called out, "Bessie, come see who decided to come into town and see us."

"Tom, do I look like I got time to run over there to see who's ridin' in?" Bessie called back, even as she wiped her hands on the towel she had in her hands and walked towards the door.

"Bessie, you know darn well you wanna know. That's why you're headed this way." Tom laughed, as he watched the woman approach.

"Oh hush. Well, look who it is!" Her hand was up and excitedly waving at the family. "Hello there..." she said loudly, as the wagon pulled up to the hitching post.

"Bessie, Tom, how ya'll doin'?" Rayne jumped down to tether the horse, reached for Ben.

Tom walked up and helped Lisbet down, then pulled her into a big hug. "Howdy, Lisbet, you're lookin' fine today. What brings you all into town?" He shared the smile he reserved for friends and family.

Rayne smiled, as she walked around with Ben in her arms. "Tom, you makin' eyes at my wife?"

"Well, Rayne, she is a very attractive woman, and you keep her out at your place away from all of us. So, when I get a chance to admire her beauty I'm gonna." Tom winked at Lisbet, who blushed slightly.

"Now, you two stop that, you're embarrassin' Lisbet. Not to mention keepin' me from seein' that there handsome boy." Bessie pushed her way to Ben and reached for the raven-haired boy.

"Hey, wait a minute, ain't ya gonna give me a hug?" Rayne feigned hurt feelings.

"Oh Lord, you just cain't stand anyone other than you gettin' any attention. Can ya?" Bessie laughed, as she wrapped the tall, dark-headed woman in a loving hug. "I cain't tell ya how much I've missed ya," she whispered into Rayne's ear, her voice shaky with emotion.

"I know, I'm sorry Bessie," Rayne whispered back, as she hugged the woman tight. Bessie had been one of the first people Rayne had met when she arrived in Willow Springs. Bessie, along with Tom, Mark Benson and his wife, Emily, welcomed her to town. They supported her and helped her when she lost Emma, the first woman she ever gave her heart to. This town would always be her home and these people her family.

Bessie cleared her throat and pulled away. "Now come on, let me get to that boy. I wanna see how big he's gotten. Mercy, look at you, why ain't you the spittin' image of your ma here. Lisbet you come on over here and give me a hug too."

"What brings you folks into town, not that we ain't happy to see ya," Tom asked as he approached.

"Well, Tom, I thought I'd bring Lisbet and Ben in for a visit, maybe some supper, and...well... Truth is, I got a favor to ask of you and Mark." Rayne pushed her black Stetson back a tad.

"Is that right? Well, you know I'm always here for ya. All ya gotta do is ask. I'm pretty sure that ol' Mark feels the same way. Why don't you head on into the dining room with Bessie, and I'll go fetch him," Tom pulled off his hat and scratched his head.

"Sounds fine. Thank ya, Tom. Maybe you could stop and fetch Sally and Emily. We'd be mighty pleased if ya joined us for supper too."

"Why, that sound's mighty fine. I'm sure Sally would love to see you, Lisbet, and Ben here. In fact, she was jawin' at me to ride out to your place and invite ya to supper. I just ain't had a chance to." He nodded and placed his hat back on his head. "I'll go fetch Mark."

"Ya'll come in here and let me get ya tea," Bessie said loudly. "This young man is tellin' me he ain't had a lick of anything to drink in hours."

"Is that so?" Rayne laughed. "That young man just knows that he has you wrapped around his little finger." She wrapped her arm around her wife's waist, and together they followed the plump woman into the dining room.

Chapter Five

With the planting and arrangements that Rayne had to make for her ranch and family, they departed Willow Springs much later than she had intended. It was midsummer when Rayne and Eunice finally arrived in Colorado.

During weeks spent either in a wagon train or on railways, Rayne saw buffalo and beautiful scenery. They made it up the San Juan Mountains to Telluride, where they finally arrived at Eunice's house. To Rayne's mind, Eunice's was a very nice home and something akin to the one she planned to make sure she had for Lisbet when she got to town.

Rayne walked to town and enquired about ranches in the area for sale but had no luck in finding anything, again. It was the piano music and laughter drifting from the building that eventually caught Rayne's attention. Well, that and the prospect of a shot of whiskey enticed her. Inside, men sat at round tables playing cards and drinking whiskey, or standing in front of the bar nursing their drinks. Upstairs, men were enjoying the company of saloon girls, spending their hard-earned pay on a good time.

Rayne had been in town for three months and once again found herself at a table nursing her drink, one eye on the door and the other on the poker game to her left. Trouble was brewing, she could feel it. She hated that she would always get a sense when trouble was likely. Suddenly, she pushed back her chair and stood up. With her black hat pulled over her eyes, she walked up to Josie, one of the many working girls, who was standing in a bad spot at the bar should a bullet go astray. Rayne whispered in her ear, "I want ya to quietly move towards the stairs and stay there." The woman turned as if to question her. "Josie, don't argue with me, just go." Rayne watched as the woman moved, and got the barkeep's attention. "Jonas, if I were you, I'd move closer to that there shotgun ya got hidin' back there."

"Mathews, what the hell ya talkin' about?" the man behind the bar asked in irritation, as he wiped the glass he held in his hand.

"I hope to hell I'm wrong, but I been watchin' Cyrus playin' with that stranger. Unless I'm missin' my guess, Cyrus is gonna get himself shot. You can keep that from happenin'."

"Now, why the hell would he be doin' that?" Jonas asked, as he stretched his neck to peer over Rayne's shoulder. "I don't think you know what the hell you're talkin' about," he finished with a laugh.

"Yup, well thanks for the whiskey," she said, as she shook her head in disappointment and tossed two bits on the bar. "Miz Martha, how's about we head on upstairs?" she spoke to the brunette who stood to her right. Rayne reached for her arm and began leading her towards the steps. They had just reached the bottom step, when Cyrus Granger pushed his chair back and shouted, "You're a low-down cheat," as he drew his gun. A shot sounded and a few women screamed, as Cyrus slowly looked down to the spreading warmth of blood from his chest and collapsed to the floor, dead.

"I don't take kindly to bein' called a cheat. Anyone else have that opinion of me?" The man stood and placed his smoking .45 on the table.

Rayne suspected that no one moved because no one felt they would be faster than the stranger. Hell, she wasn't sure she would be fast enough. Well, that and they weren't sure that the stranger was cheating. Cyrus had a problem with whiskey, and when he was losing and losing a lot, everyone was a cheater. Fortunately, most of the locals knew this and knew when to just walk away.

The sheriff rushed in after hearing the gunshot. "Someone wanna tell me what the hell just happened here?"

"Well, Sheriff, this man here felt I was cheatin' him and was gonna draw on me. I just happen to be faster. And no, I wasn't cheatin', he was just a lousy player. So, I suppose I'm the cause of the commotion."

"Jonas, is that true?" the sheriff asked, turning his steely gaze to the barkeep.

"Sheriff, it seems to be the case…I mean, I cain't say that I was payin' much attention, but Cyrus did push outta his chair yellin' about bein' cheated. Mathews there may know more about it than I do."

"Um-hmm, that sound right with all you gentlemen that was playin' with this stranger?" The sheriff asked the group of men who had jumped away from the table when the dead man first shouted. Murmurs of agreement came from several men, as well as a couple of the girls that had been near the table.

"Well then, I suppose it was a case of self-defense, but mister, I suggest you get on your horse and get out of town. Don't much like killin' in my town."

The man carefully reached for his gun and holstered it and went to gather the pile of coins and the few bills that lay on the table.

"No sir, the money stays," came the deep voice of the sheriff, whose eyes were fixed on the man who was dressed a might fancier than anyone else in the room. Men dressed like that were usually bad news as far as he was concerned. In a mining town, he had enough bad news with local men, he didn't need it from a stranger.

"Alright, I suppose I'll be headin' off then. Thank ya'll for the game. I'm sorry it ended this way." The man reached for his hat and stood. He placed the hat on his head and pulled down the bottom of his fancy vest. He reached for his suit jacket and slipped it on, then walked out the swinging doors to his horse.

The bar started to settle back to normal. Jonas shouted, "Drinks on the house," and quickly, the mood shifted. The men were back to spending money, even as Cyrus's body was carried out.

Rayne whispered, "Miz Martha, you alright? Maybe headin' upstairs ain't such a good idea anymore. Let me at least buy ya a drink."

"Mathews, can I have a word with ya?" the sheriff asked, as he took the few steps to the staircase.

"Jesus, how do I get myself into these messes?" she muttered, quietly.

"Excuse me, did ya say somethin' there? I couldn't quite hear ya."

Rayne plastered a half smile on her face and spoke louder, "Uh, no sir, I didn't say a thing. Let me just get Miz Martha here a drink first."

"Jonas, give the lady a drink. Well look there, looks like Miz Martha is bein' taken care of. Now, how about that talk?" Sheriff Hawks said with a tone of authority in his voice.

Rayne gave a slight nod of acceptance and led the way to a table in the corner and took a seat. The sheriff followed and took a seat himself.

"So, Sheriff, what can I do for ya?" Rayne asked, as she took a deep breath and mentally prepared herself for the questions.

"I know you're new to town and that you're a friend of Eunice's. Other than that, I don't know much about ya. But I want ya to know that I don't cotton much to trouble, and there is just somethin' about you that I ain't sure about."

"Such as?" Rayne asked, as she looked straight into the man's eyes. She knew she was being sized up and was walking a thin line. Hell, if she were in the sheriff's shoes, she would do the same thing. She didn't like lying to people, but she also knew it was an easier world for men than it was for women.

"Well, for instance, take Miz Martha there…I seen ya was headin' upstairs, yet ya decide to buy her a drink instead. And from what I hear, ya never really do make it to a room up there. For a single man, ya don't seem too eager for their company. Why is that?"

"Well, I get tongue tied. I seem to forget how to talk when a woman is around," Rayne said, hoping she sounded convincing.

"Ya don't seem to have that problem with Eunice. Now why is that?" the sheriff asked.

He was curious about the town's newest inhabitant. He wasn't sure what it was about Rayne, but whatever it was brought out his protective instincts. Clinton Hawks wasn't normally a protective kind of man. In fact, even with his own son he seldom showed any kind of protectiveness, yet he couldn't deny the feelings. Hawks was in his late forties, with compassionate eyes that saw more than he let on.

"Eunice is nice. She don't judge, and she don't pry," Rayne spoke, looking at the floor.

"I ain't one to judge, son," Hawks said, as he shrugged his shoulders. "I reckon iffin at some point you'll start trustin' folks around here...least I hope you'll find you can trust me. When ya do, I'll be ready to listen. But for the time bein', I sure could use some help keepin' the peace. I understand you want to start a ranch around these parts. I could maybe help introduce ya to some folks. Until then, I sure wouldn't mind havin' you as a deputy. You got grit and a keen eye for trouble. Will ya consider my offer?"

"Well, I won't lie, I could use some money, and folks ain't jumpin' to offer advice on the property around here. Maybe with a word from you some might become friendlier," Rayne said thoughtfully.

"Hell, son, folks around here tend to be suspicious of strangers. Everyone wants to steal their claim. Ya know?" Hawks laughed. "Come on over to my office, and I'll get ya a badge. I reckon ya know how to use those irons ya got strapped to your hip."

"Yes sir, I do. Though I ain't proud of it." He saw a change in those dark eyes; it was subtle but there none the same. It was a look of regret or guilt. It was the look a person had when they had taken a life and felt remorse for it. It was a look that told him Rayne respected life and didn't jump to using the Colts that were strapped to his hip. Rayne was the kind of man he wanted on his side of the law. Yup, he knew he'd made a good choice in approaching Rayne. With a little luck, he would get to know Rayne better and find out what it was that made him feel the way he did.

"Come on, son. Let's go get your badge, and I'll walk ya around town and introduce ya to folks. You can get an idea of who's friendly and who's full of shit. Then I'll bring ya back here, buy you a drink, and you and Miz Martha can...well...we'll see what happens."

With a smile, Rayne stood. "Alright, a job sounds mighty fine. I gotta say, I'm kinda tired of sittin' around watchin' these gentlemen play cards."

"Yup, I reckon that gets somewhat borin' after a while. But then again, sometimes bein' a lawman ain't any more exciting. Course, there's times that ya get more excitement than ya bargain for. You ain't got any aversion to shootin' do ya?"

"No sir, I ain't. I'll shoot when I gotta. I ain't yellow, but I ain't wild about killin' a man either."

"That's all I needed to know," Hawks said, as they walked out of the saloon.

†

A few hours later, Deputy Mathews walked out of the sheriff's office and headed towards the stable with a big grin on her face and a badge pinned to her vest. Her ride was short, and she soon dismounted. With a spring in her step and whistling a tune, she walked through the gate and straight to the door of a white house. She opened the door and hollered, "Eunice, I got me a job!"

Eunice walked in from the kitchen. She was red faced, with a smudge of flour on her cheek, and wiping her hands on a dish towel. "What are you hollerin' about?" Eunice asked as she smiled, then stopped in her tracks as she spotted the badge.

"I got a job; I'm the new deputy. How's about that?"

Eunice quickly regained the smile that had faltered. "Isn't that nice, but aren't you afraid of getting shot or well…" Eunice paused, frowned, then continued, "you've been in disguise, and if the sheriff knew, I don't think he'd take much kindly to being duped."

"Sheriff Hawks seems to be a reasonable man. I aim to be straight with him soon enough," Rayne said. She just needed to get a little money saved up and a few folks to give her more than a suspicious look every time she walked into the mercantile or saloon. "Somethin' smells good, what's for supper?"

Eunice walked to the window and looked out. "I have a chicken roasting. I was planning on some boiled potatoes, and I'm mixing up biscuits."

Rayne watched Eunice carefully. "Whatcha lookin' at? You expectin' someone?"

"As a matter of fact, my husband is supposed to be getting in, anytime now. I'm hoping he gets home in time for supper." The brunette turned to face Rayne and smiled. "Would you like a drink before supper?"

"Sounds good. So tell me more about Harry. You really don't talk much about him, how come?"

"I don't?" Eunice said in surprise. "Well, what do you want to know?"

"Well, what's he do for a livin'?" Rayne took the drink Eunice offered and sat down in a parlor chair.

"Harry...well, Harry is a jack of all trades, and he knows some about farming, mining, gambling. He's done some ranching too. I think you two would get along just fine. He's a sweet man, you know, caring and kind."

"So where's he been, and why does he let you travel alone?"

"He doesn't. Why do you say that?" Eunice asked.

"Cuz he does. You was travelin' alone when ya came upon my ranch, and you fully planned on travelin' here alone. And he wasn't here when we arrived. So where's he been?"

"He's actually been on a cattle buying trip," Eunice replied distractedly. "I need to go finish the biscuits, wanna come help?"

"Sure, I suppose you'll need someone to peel them potatoes." Rayne laughed. "I bet Harry ain't never had to worry about bein' asked to peel potatoes... Lord knows, Lisbet asks me to do that often enough."

"Oh, don't kid yourself, Harry pitches in as well. Course he wouldn't be admitting that to anyone." Eunice laughed and headed back towards the kitchen.

Just as Eunice was setting supper on the table, she heard the door open and saw Harry walk in. With a big smile on her face, she set the platter of chicken down, ran to Harry, and jumped into his arms.

"Easy there, darlin', ya might wanna let a man get his bearin's first," Harry said, as laughter came rumbling from deep down inside.

Eunice wrapped her arms around Harry's neck, as his arms wrapped around her waist. "Lord, I missed you," she whispered seconds before he claimed her lips.

The kiss had just started, when Rayne walked out from the kitchen with a plate full of biscuits and the mashed potatoes. "Ya wanna get the gravy so we can get started? I'm starvin' and this here meal smells great." She came to a stop when her eyes caught the scene at the door.

The strong arms set Eunice back on her feet, and blue eyes focused on Rayne and the badge pinned to the vest.

"You wanna tell me who the hell you are and what you're doin' in my house?" Harry said, as his hand slowly moved to the butt of his gun. "Etta, wanna tell me why the hell there's a lawman in my house?"

"Harry, this here is my friend, Rayne." Eunice answered quickly, her hand reaching for his gun hand.

"Hmm, that still don't tell me why he's in my house."

"Well, Rayne has been staying here with me since we got to town, and Rayne ain't exactly a man..." Eunice rushed on. "Rayne Mathews, this is my husband, Harry. Harry this is Rayne. She and Lisbet were kind enough to take me in while I was traveling and got stuck in storms, back in Wisconsin. Rayne and Lisbet want to expand their ranch, and I thought you'd be the perfect one to show me the area. And well, Rayne needed a job, and Sheriff Hawks needed a deputy, so it was good timing. Come on, Harry, supper is getting cold. Rayne, how about you grab the gravy and we all sit down?" Eunice led Harry to the seat at the head of the table.

Harry followed reluctantly as he was pulled towards the table. He tossed his hat on a chair as he passed. He'd missed Eunice, was starving, tired, and in need of a bath and soft bed. However, walking into his home and seeing a lawman was the last thing he'd expect or trust. But Eunice said this person was her friend, and for now, he would trust that. "Sure does smell good." He pulled out his chair and sat down.

Eunice leaned down and kissed his cheek and whispered, "Thank you," before she sat down in her own seat and smiled at Rayne as she walked in with the gravy and joined them.

Harry placed his elbows on the table and steepled his fingers in front of him, his gaze switching between Rayne and Eunice.

"So, Harry, why don't ya relax some. Eunice and I are just friends," Rayne said calmly, as she dished herself a spoonful of potatoes and passed them to the man on her left.

"You find Etta not to your likin'?" Harry bristled a tad.

"Harry…" Eunice replied quickly,

"Eunice, could you please pass the chicken? It smells great, and I'm starvin'." Rayne flashed a big smile at the woman. "Harry, I never said she ain't to my likin'. Fact is, I never looked at her that way. She's an attractive woman indeed, however, I got me a wife and son in Wisconsin. Right now, I need to put all my energy into gettin' a place for 'em."

"Is that right?" Harry asked as he eyed Rayne. "Well, that makes all the difference then don't it." He faked a smile and reached for the chicken. "Etta honey, how about you get me a drink of whiskey?"

Eunice stood up and walked to the buffet table where there sat a decanter of amber liquid and a set of matching glasses. She took the top off the decanter and poured a glass. "Rayne, would you like one as well?" When Rayne declined, Eunice set it down and walked back to the table. She placed the glass in front of Harry and took her seat again and picked up her fork.

"Harry, I got this naggin' feelin' that I've seen you somewhere. I just cain't place where." Rayne held her fork full of mashed potatoes halfway to her mouth.

"Can't say I've ever met ya before. Course might have been my twin." Harry laughed.

Rayne joined in with a chuckle as well. "Yup that could be so."

"I hear you callin' Eunice by the name Etta? How come?"

"Ah hell, it ain't nothin' but a nickname. I'm surprised she didn't tell ya." Harry turned and looked at Eunice. "Why didn't ya tell Rayne your nickname?"

"Well, honestly, I just didn't think about it," Eunice responded before she took a sip of her lemonade. "I'm sorry Rayne, you can call me Etta if you'd like."

Rayne flashed a real big smile. "I'd like that! Makes me feel real special to be included in your group of friends."

Harry held up his glass. "Here's to new friends."

Rayne smiled and reached for her glass of lemonade. "To new friends."

Harry did relax a tad once Etta invited the stranger to call her by her name. After dinner dishes were done, Rayne said goodnight and went upstairs to her room.

Once Rayne was in her room and settled, she wrote a letter to Lisbet to tell her about the job.

My dearest,

It's hard to believe I've been gone for three months already and that winter is just around the corner. God, I miss you and Ben. Looks like my stay here is gonna be a little longer than I expected. Folks around here are mighty suspicious of strangers, afraid someone's gonna steal their claim I reckon. But I think I got an in now seein that I was just hired as the new deputy here in town. I believe now folks will open up and get to know me, be willin to show me around to some of the properties around here. Let me tell you, there is some beautiful land here. Prime land for cattle. I'm prayin that by springtime I'll have a place and will be able to have you and Ben join me.

It'll help too that Eunice's husband Harry is back in town. Seems like a decent fellow, but you know, I got this naggin feelin that I seen him somewhere before. Then there's the fact that he calls Eunice Etta. Says it's a nickname or something. I gotta say though, I think it fits her better than Eunice.

Damn Lisbet, I can't tell you how much I miss you. Sometimes I swear I'm gonna go outta my mind for missin you so much. I miss your smile and your laugh. I knew it was gonna be bad, just not this bad. I miss the little things you know, like did you know that when you're thinkin real hard or frustrated, you play with a strand of hair? You twist it round and round your finger, Lord I miss seein you do that.

I've also been thinkin a lot about those days and nights before Eunice and I left. I swear there are times I can taste you on my lips, I smell your scent on my skin. A combination of lavender and honeysuckle. Your skin's so soft and smooth, I don't think I ever felt anythin as soft as you, darlin. Lord, just the memory of your touch, gets my blood goin, and honestly, you is pretty much all I been thinkin of.

I close my eyes when my head hits the pillow and there you are, your beautiful face so close I can reach out and touch it, my fingertips feel your soft, warm skin. Your eyes sparklin. Your mouth, your lips so invitin all full and just beggin to be kissed. If I listen hard enough, I can hear your breathin change. I can hear your heart start beatin faster, and I can see your eyes darken, the way they do when you want me. I feel your hands touchin my body, and how it reacts to your touch. I can feel the way yours reacts to my touch. Lord, I miss that. I miss the way your body feels movin against mine and the way you whimper when you just can't get enough of me. The way you take me with you when you finally reach your release and I feel your love coat me. It's heaven, my darlin, and I truly can't wait to feel you in my arms again. I pray it comes soon.

I'm gonna say good night now, my love, need to get some sleep. I got a big day tomorrow. First official day of bein the new deputy. Wish me luck, darlin. Know that my love is bein sent with this, and with God's will, it won't be much longer until you and Ben are with me, and we are once again a family.

With my deepest love and devotion,
Rayne

Rayne folded the paper, slipped it into an envelope, and sealed it, intent on getting it to the post office the next day. She stood up and walked over to the open window of her room. As she leaned against the window frame with her hands in her pockets, she felt the cool breeze and looked up at the darkened sky. She could see the stars against the night sky so clearly that she felt she could reach out and touch them. She took a deep breath of the fresh, cool air and let the calmness of the surrounding mountains and meadows settle in her. This was almost perfect; the only things missing were Lisbet and Ben. Once they were all together in their new home, her life would be complete. With a touch of loneliness, she walked back into her room and closed the door. She walked towards the bed, as she unbuttoned her shirt and removed the binding that held her breasts flat, giving her the appearance of a man. She hated that she couldn't live her life as the person she was, but this world belonged to men. Maybe someday, she hoped, that would change.

Rayne changed into her sleeping gown and climbed into the bed. She pulled up the covers and closed her eyes. With thoughts of Lisbet, she drifted off to sleep.

✝

Harry sat on the bed with his back against the headboard, his legs crossed at the ankles, and fingers laced behind his head. His eyes were on Etta as she brushed her hair. "So, a lawman livin' in our house. Tell me again how that happened." Sitting there watching her, he just couldn't concentrate on anything but how beautiful she was.

Etta paused mid stroke, as she glanced at Harry's reflection in her mirror. With a smile, she placed the brush on her vanity and slowly swung around in the seat, her robe opening to reveal a well-toned, creamy calf. Her hands were slowly moving to the v of the robe, between her breasts. "Honestly, Harry, you really wanna discuss that right now?" Her voice was like honey, and her eyes looked him up and down. She glided to her feet and slowly walked towards the bed, dropping the robe as she walked.

Harry swallowed hard and growled. "No, I don't believe I do…" He drew her into his arms as she reached the side of the bed.

Chapter Six

Maddie Tomlinson leaned against the bar, a hand on her hip and a smile on her lips, as she surveyed the saloon. With red ringlets cascading over her shoulders and falling down the straps of the green gown that barely contained her breasts, she captured the eye of most men in the room. She was never at a loss for the company, should she desire it. Today though, there was only one person she sought out, and that person wasn't in the saloon. She knew it wouldn't be long before she laid eyes on the tall deputy.

Rayne strolled down the boardwalk. The black brim of her hat shaded her eyes from the bright sun. A black duster hung from her shoulders, keeping the slight chill from touching her. Every now and then, she would touch the brim of her hat at a passing lady, or say hello to one of the many miners or ranchers that passed her. She was finally finding her place in this community, making friends, and finally had a lead on some property she was interested in. For her, all the pieces were finally falling into place. Etta and Harry had indeed turned out to be great friends. A few days after she started as deputy of the town, she had been looking through wanted posters when she realized why Harry looked so familiar to her. She had seen his wanted poster back in Willow Springs, in Tom's office. Harry was none other than the partner of Butch Cassidy. She had asked Clinton about Harry and the fact that he was an outlaw.

"Mathews, old Harry and Butch are good fellas. They ain't never done anything in this town and are friends of mine. Iffin' ya got a problem with that and ya might be thinkin' of talkin' to them Pinkertons, maybe ya should turn your badge in and reconsider settin' roots down in these parts. Around here, they're good folks, and there ain't a body here that'd cotton to anyone messin' with 'em." Clinton said, as he leaned forward in his chair.

"Na, I ain't got a problem with Harry. Hell, I was just askin'. Both he and Eunice, I mean Etta, have been decent folks to me. Hell, Etta offered a roof over my head and a place at her table. For me, that's all that matters."

It wasn't until she said it that she realized it was true. She really didn't care that Harry ran with a bank robber. The fact of the matter was, they didn't kill anyone during the commission of their robberies, and from what she could see, Harry was a decent man. He cared about Etta and was quick to lend a hand to his neighbors. She'd been around enough to know that people were usually more than the labels others put on them.

It was the piano music and laughter that drew her out of her thoughts. With a smile, she walked in. Standing at the swinging doors, she waited for her eyes to adjust then scanned the room. With a big smile and a nod, she headed for a table of card players with an open seat. "Howdy fella's, ya'll keepin' out of trouble?" she asked as she approached.

"Shoot, Deputy, Trouble is my middle name," one of the men replied.

The group of men laughed, then one asked, "Ya got time for a game, Deputy?"

"Ya got money to lose do ya, Horace?" Rayne laughed. "I reckon I can play a hand or two." She pulled out the chair and sat down.

"Let me tell ya, I think I hit a vein. It's lookin' good, so yeah I got me some money!" Horace replied, his big smile revealed discolored, crooked teeth, and his usually dull-gray eyes were twinkling.

Rayne immediately grew alert. She glanced around, her eyes taking in anyone close enough to have heard Horace's statement. Announcing in a crowded bar that you've hit a vein in a mining town was a sure way to make yourself a target. And it was her job to make sure Horace didn't come to any harm while he was in town. "Now, ya ought to be careful about announcin' that. Ya never know who's listenin'," Rayne replied, as she pushed her hat back.

"Hell, Deputy, I'll lose it all one way or nother..." Horace replied, as he lifted his glass of whiskey to his mouth.

Antes were made and cards dealt, hands were won and lost, and the girls in the room were occasionally pulling men away. Maddie was no different. Rayne knew Maddie was watching her. She'd tried hard to get Rayne upstairs, and even though Rayne didn't take her up on the offer to leave the table, she didn't leave Rayne's shoulder. And that's how the afternoon passed. It was late afternoon when Rayne finally stood and announced that she needed to make her rounds. She thanked the men at the table and collected her winnings. Maddie, of course, wasn't happy that her attentions were being ignored and she loudly said, "Now, Deputy, I'm not sure how I should take the fact that you'd much rather play cards than spend time with me."

Rayne turned to Maddie and replied, "Well now, Miz Maddie, I by no means meant to offend you. Let me buy ya a drink, and I'll try and come back after my rounds, how's that sound?" Her smile never reached her blue eyes.

Maddie smiled as she walked up to Rayne and placed her arm on the strong shoulder. Her fingertips stroking the back of Rayne's neck, she replied, "Oh, I suppose I can forgive you if ya promise to come back."

Rayne reached for the arm that was on her shoulder and lifted it off. "All I can say is I'll try. I wouldn't want to promise and then break it for some unknown reason. That just ain't right to do, ya know? Now, the sooner I get goin', the sooner I may be able to get back. Jonas, will you give Miz Maddie here a whiskey and put it on my tab?" She headed for the swinging doors.

Rayne walked around the boardwalk, up one side and down the other, and stopped at the mercantile where she leaned against the outside wall, her eyes on the doorway of the saloon. It wasn't long before a drunk Horace stumbled out and went for his horse. He managed to get up in the saddle and set his mount towards his shack and the small claim he held. Rayne walked a few steps to her own horse, her eyes still on the saloon doors. Just as she thought, a couple of strangers in town walked out with purpose, jumped on their horses, and spurred them in the direction Horace had headed. "God damn it, Horace," she muttered, as she got on her own horse to follow.

†

Had Rayne not been worried about Horace and feared for his safety, she would have loved the view of the valley below. But she had to keep her eyes on the trail; she needed to be careful that neither of the men had hung back out of sight to make sure they weren't followed.

The sun was low in the sky when she sighted the shack hidden by trees. She heard a gunshot. She jumped off her horse as she drew her.45 and took cover behind a big tree, her eyes never leaving the front of the shack. As the two men ran out of the shack with saddle bags in their hands, she took aim at one and got off a clean shot. The second man spun around, with his saddle bag still in his hand, and ran towards the mine shaft. Rayne gave chase.

She crouched down as she hit the opening of the mine. As her eyes adjusted, her ears picked up the echo of running footsteps and then nothing but silence. With her heart pounding, she slowly made her way deeper into the mine, guided by the faint light of torches placed in spots throughout the tunnel. She came to a fork. She stopped, hoping to be able to hear something that would tell her which way to go.

After a few seconds of deliberation, she ventured down one passageway and soon came to a dead end. She turned around and backtracked; she knew that it was getting late and the chance of finding the man in the tunnels was slim. She should get back to outside and check on Horace, though she knew in her heart he was gone.

She made her way out of the mine and ran to the entrance of the shack. Her fear was confirmed when she found Horace's body sprawled on the floor near the small wood stove. Swearing, she walked back outside to the body that lay on the ground. She got the body on the horse that nosed around the ground and whistled for her own mount, keeping her eyes and ears alert for any sound that would indicate the other man had made his way out of the mine. With the reins of the second horse tethered to her saddle, she climbed up and started the trek back to town. She was halfway down the mountain, when a shot rang out and knocked her off her horse.

As she hit the ground, her head struck a rock, and she lost consciousness. When she came to, her head ached and her shoulder throbbed. She was dizzy and, as she brought her hand up to her shoulder, she could feel blood still seeping from the wound. She needed to stop the bleeding, so she patted the pockets of her duster and found a handkerchief in one of the pockets. She reached in with her left hand and pulled it out. Through breaths of pain and gritted teeth, she reached up to her right shoulder and pushed the material hard against the wound. Immediately, her forehead beaded with sweat and her head spun.

She closed her eyes in an effort to keep her churning stomach from emptying. She opened her eyes to the light of the moon and saw the horses walking back towards her. "Oh thank God," Rayne muttered and gently whistled for the horse. "Come on...yeah, that's right." The simple noise caused her head to throb. With a lot of effort, she finally made it up onto the horse and gently spoke to the animal, "Oh boy, I'm gonna trust that you know the way home. How about it, wanna take me home?"

Maddie had stepped out into the cool air, when she saw the horses approaching. She turned towards the entrance and shouted, "Someone run get the doc and tell the sheriff we got a wounded man here." She ran to the horses and caught the reins just as Rayne fell off her horse. Several men ran up and were taking the reins and pulling the dead man off the back of the animal. The doc dashed out and knelt down to examine the fallen deputy. "We need to get him warm and somewhere I can get a better look at his wounds."

Maddie replied tersely, "My room's the closest, take him there." Maddie pushed a path through the crowd, as a couple of men helped carry Rayne upstairs to the room. Once Rayne was placed in the bed, the doc cleared everyone out, except for Maddie, who insisted on staying to help.

The doc cut away Rayne's shirt and the binding that held her breasts flat. Without a word, he went to work to remove the bullet that was still in Rayne's shoulder.

Maddie kept a neutral expression on her face, but was smiling to herself; she had just known that Rayne wasn't who she pretended to be, and it intrigued her even more. *Oh Rayne, do I have plans for us.*

It was close to an hour later when the doctor and Maddie finally descended the stairs to a crowded room.

"Is my deputy gonna be alright?" Hawks asked solemnly.

"Took the bullet out and finally got the bleedin' stopped. She's gonna be weak, lost a lot of blood, but I'm optimistic. I am worried about her head wound, though. But ain't nothin' I can do till she wakes up."

A low murmur went through the room when the crowd heard that the deputy was a woman, then whoops of happiness erupted in the saloon, and smiles appeared on the faces of the miners as they heard the deputy would be fine.

The doctor walked over to the sheriff. "Did you know?" he asked, as he reached for the shot of whiskey the sheriff handed him.

"Yup, Mathews confided in me a couple weeks ago. Asked me to keep her secret, and I did. Hell, if she can do the job, what difference does it make? Folks have taken to her, and she's good people."

"That's what I was hopin' you'd say. How about the other rider?"

"From what the fella's here are tellin' me, he and another fella were passin' through. They stopped for a couple of beers and were playin' cards with Horace earlier. Horace was jawin' about havin' made a strike. I asked for a couple of volunteers to go out to Horace's and check on him. They should be back by mornin'."

"Well, I'm thinkin' it ain't gonna be good, what with the deputy and a dead man ridin' in like they did."

"Yup, I know. Keep an eye on Mathews and let me know soon as she wakes up." Hawks drank his whiskey then headed for the swinging doors.

Once outside, he said under his breath, "God damn it, Horace, what the hell were you thinkin'?"

He headed towards Harry and Etta's place; he needed to tell them about their friend.

✝

Maddie sat in the chair that she pulled close to the bed. She wiped the beads of sweat from Rayne's forehead, wrung the cloth in the basin, wiped Rayne's brow, and paced the floor.

When Rayne did finally stir it was to kick at the blankets and ramble incoherent words. It was close to the next evening before she opened her eyes and glanced around the room.

Rayne spotted Maddie in a chair. She closed her eyes and passed out again.

The next thing she felt was the doc examining her shoulder. The pain was enough to bring her out of sleep and cause her to be in a foul mood. "Jesus Christ. I swear if ya poke at me one more time I'm gonna shove my fist down your throat and pull your guts right up outta your mouth," she shouted. The shout startled Doc Granger enough that he jumped, and Maddie dropped the pitcher of water she had in her hands. Rayne didn't know what hurt more, the doc poking at her or the noise of the pitcher hitting the floor and shattering.

After the momentary surprise, Doc stepped closer to Rayne and spoke, "Well, I suppose that's a clear sign that you're still with us."

"Considerin' the pain in my head, I would beg to differ with ya. Where the hell am I?" Rayne groaned, fighting nausea in her stomach.

Maddie, who had been cleaning up the broken porcelain walked to the side of the bed. She glanced at the doc with a questioning look in her eyes and carefully began to say, "Rayne, honey, you're in my room. Do you remember ridin' into town last night?"

"Rayne, can ya open your eyes for me?" Doc Granger spoke.

Rayne complied, even though the light from the lantern caused her head to explode. Doc looked into her eyes and carefully felt the back of her head. "Can ya tell me your name?"

"Can I close my eyes? The light is killin' me."

"Of course. Tell me everything ya remember."

"Well, my name is Rayne Mathews, I'm a deputy here in town, and I think I rode into town with a dead man slung over his horse. Yeah, there was a shootout up on the mountain."

"Right, what else do you remember?" Maddie asked, "Do you remember me?"

"Well, of course, I remember you, Maddie, what kinda fool question is that?" Rayne asked, her patience dwindling.

"It's alright Rayne, get some rest. We'll talk later," Doc Granger said, as he motioned Maddie to follow him.

†

Once out in the hall, Doc spoke, "She looks like she's gonna be alright. It's gonna take some time for her to heal, but right now, I don't see anything to indicate any infection. I'd like ya to keep an eye on her cuz of that bump on her head. She's gonna have a headache for a couple of days, but that should start to lessen soon. Make sure she don't move the arm and cause any more bleedin'. She's gonna need to rest in bed a few more days."

"Alright, I'll take care of her, Doc."

"Maddie, behave yourself. Mathews is gonna need time to heal."

With an incredulous look on her face and an indignant tone, she responded, "I can't believe you would imply that I'd do anything other than care for Rayne."

"Maddie, I know you and see that look in your eye when you see Mathews walk in. The image of a hungry wolf about to devour a wounded animal comes to mind."

With a huff, Maddie spun on her heel, reached for the door knob, and hastily walked back into her room.

Chapter Seven

For Rayne, the next couple of days all drifted together, and her headache slowly eased as her shoulder healed. Maddie took care of her. One day, as Maddie was re-bandaging the wound, Rayne asked, "Maddie, how come you're doin' all this?"

The redhead turned her eyes from the wound and looked into the dark-haired woman's blue eyes. With a tilt of her head, she replied softly, "Well, because it's what you do for someone you love. Rayne, do you remember anything about our relationship?"

Rayne blushed slightly, cleared her throat, and hesitated. "Well, honestly, not a whole lot. I mean I remember I was supposed to come see ya the night I was shot, kinda feel like I was comin' to court ya. Was I?"

"That's right," exclaimed Maddie. "You and me, we got feelin's for each other, and well, there's folks in town that would rather us not be together. But you were slowly makin' your intentions known." Maddie's hand was gently touching Rayne's arm.

"Who...who don't want us together?" Rayne asked, confused. "I mean, I know it ain't exactly conventional and all but, if we love each other, ain't no one got the right to tell us any different."

"I know, darlin', now don't go getting yourself all upset. It really don't matter who, as long as you remember you love me and want to be with me, that's all that matters."

"I wanna know who. Friends of mine?" Rayne pushed. She was frustrated with the pounding in her head. While it was easing up, it still hurt more often than not. She was frustrated that she was still weak and not able to be up and moving around as she wanted, and she was extremely frustrated that she couldn't really remember much of her life before arriving in town the night she had been shot.

Sure, she remembered the basics; she knew her name, knew she was the deputy; she had vague flashes of memories of a cabin in the mountains, a shootout; she recognized some faces and could match names but had no real memory of how she knew them or their relationship. Some of the things she heard and was told made sense, but other than hearing about them, she had no way of knowing if they were true. She felt like she was missing a big part of herself, and she didn't know what it was or how to find it.

"Rayne ..."

"Who, damn it? I wanna know," Rayne shouted, instantly regretting her actions, as her head pounded.

"Well, Etta for one and Harry, though he is just saying that so he and Etta don't fight," Maddie replied, as she dropped her eyes.

"Thank you for tellin' me. If ya don't mind, I need to close my eyes."

"Of course, I'm done with your bandages anyway. You get some rest, and I'll make sure you have some supper when you wake up." Maddie stood and gathered the dirty bandages and washbasin then slipped quietly out the door.

In the hallway, she came face to face with Etta.

"How's Rayne today?" Etta asked.

"I'm sorry Etta, but the deputy is still really weak. There isn't much improvement yet, and the doc says she should be left alone so's she can regain her strength," Maddie replied protectively.

"Are you sure she isn't up to seeing me? I have mail for her from back home. I think she would love to read it, or at least have me read it to her." Etta glanced at the door.

"Look, I'm just followin' the doc's orders, and he said no visitors. Give me the mail, I'll make sure she gets it." The redhead impatiently shifted the basin in her hand to reach for whatever mail Etta had.

Etta once again glanced towards the door and hesitated before she reached into her purse and pulled out the letter from Lisbet. "Alright, make sure she gets it, please."

The anger flashing in Maddie's eyes signaled her patience was stretched thin. She grabbed the letter from Etta and spat, "Well, of course, she'd get it. Now, if you don't mind, I have things to do while Rayne is sleepin'. 'Sides, I'm sure Harry will be wonderin' where you are."

Etta stiffened but politely said, "Of course, I apologize for keeping you from your duties." Then she brushed passed her.

"Etta, don't go thinkin' you're any better than me. From what I've heard, you're just like me."

Etta stopped for a split second as the comment struck its mark then continued walking down the hallway. All the while, Maddie's laughter rang in her ears.

Maddie clutched the letter in her hand, as she walked downstairs. She placed the wash basin on a counter in the back room then ripped the letter open and began to read it. While her education was lacking, she did manage to make out a few of the words written on the paper.

She jumped and hid the paper behind her back when she heard Jane. "Maddie what are ya doin' back here? Jonas ain't gonna be happy if he catches you. Ya know he's already mad that you've got the deputy up in your room and ya ain't makin' no money."

"I know he ain't happy. Hey, Jane, you got any schoolin'?"

"Some why?"

"Well, do ya know how to read?" Maddie ignored the other woman's question. Her eyes darting to the doorway behind Jane.

"Like I said, I got some," Jane approached Maddie "Whatcha got in your hands?"

"If I let ya see, ya can't tell no one. And I do mean no one."

"Lord Maddie, if ya don't wanna tell me, then don't be expectin' me to read for ya."

"Look, it's a letter for the deputy from someone back from where she came from. You know how I feel about Rayne, I…I wanna know what I'm up against."

"She's in your bed, so I don't think you got anything to worry about," Jane laughed. "Come on, let me see that letter."

Maddie handed Jane the letter she had hidden behind her back then waited for Jane to start reading.

Sweetheart,

It feels as though you've been away forever. Lord knows I miss you. I doubt ya know how much the few simple words ya write have come to mean to me or how much I look forward to them. Maybe ya do since ya tell me that you look forward to readin my letters to you. I love readin the words ya write, but it reminds me of how much I miss ya.

It's so hard without you here. I know you're workin hard to get us a home there, but sometimes I just want ya to come back home to us. I feel so torn, cuz I want ya to follow your dreams, but I want ya to follow them here with us. I know that sounds selfish, and I'm so sorry Rayne. I know you're gonna do what ya gotta do before ya come back home. Just promise me you'll come back to us, we're here waitin for ya and we ain't goin anywhere.

Ben is growin like a weed. I doubt you'd recognize him, even though it's only been a few months. I tell ya, the more he eats and grows, the more I pray that ya get this expansion goin. We'd best have plenty of plots for a garden and plenty of fattened cows.

I reckon you're chompin at the bit to hear about the ranch, and there's plenty to tell ya about.

So far, the ranch is lookin real good. We got a real good stand of crops for the cattle, and let me tell ya, it looks beautiful. If we aren't rained out, we're gonna have a nice harvest. Tom says with all the small towns poppin up along the railroads, we should have a good market for both the crops and the cattle, so we stand to make plenty of money. With that said, ya best be gettin home to work the deals.

Rayne, I do have some news that ya ain't gonna like, but ya gotta know about it. I know ya got a soft spot for John, but I had to let him go. I wish with all my heart that I didn't have to tell ya, but after ya left he changed. The way he looked at me made me uncomfortable, and honestly, he was tellin folks in town that with you gone the ranch was gonna be his. I felt like he expected you to not come back. But that ain't the worst of it. He really started drinkin and gamblin more. There were weeks that he wouldn't even bother to come back to work. And when he did, he behaved as though he didn't have to lift a finger and bossed the other hands around while he sat and smoked and drank. Now mind you, I don't mind a drink after work is done, but he was drinkin all day. I suppose the last straw was when he went to whip Ben. He said Ben had been tormentin Romeo all day long, and that wasn't true. You know Ben adores Romeo. I ain't ashamed to say, had Tom not stopped by to check on us and seen what he was about to do and stopped him, I would have killed him.

I feel like the good Lord was watchin over us. Tom was bringin Jesse over to see about work when all this happened. You know Jesse, he's Otis Jenkins's oldest boy. I don't mind tellin ya, I was glad that they was here. It took em both to keep John from actin on his anger. I got Jesse stayin in the bunk house, and I feel safer with him here. John made some threatenin comments when Tom was gettin him on his horse to take him to town. Don't worry about us. Things are handled here, and we're safe, I just felt ya needed to know.

Rayne, I miss you. I'll be fixin dinner and remember somethin Ben did earlier in the day and went to tell ya and ya ain't there. Or I'll look over at Ben playin, and I'm surprised to not see ya there with him.

The days are easiest. I suppose it's because I got so much to do. What with the daily chores and chasin after that boy of ours, I don't have time to miss you. But at night, after Ben is in his bed asleep and I got time alone for my thoughts, that's when the loneliness sets in.

Lord Rayne, I miss everything about you. The way you watch me when ya think I ain't payin attention. The smile that meets your eyes, those amazin blue eyes of yours. I miss them watchin me. I miss your strong arms holdin me and your lips as you kiss me. I go to bed at night and miss you beside me. I'll roll over and expect to feel you there and ya ain't. I pray that I'll wake up and you'll be there when my eyes open, and I'm disappointed when ya ain't. Then I remind myself that it's only for a while, and that works for the day and then it happens all over again that evenin.

Darlin, I hope you know, I ain't the only one that misses you. When Tom or Matt stops by to check on us and the door opens, Ben's face lights up cuz he's expectin it to be you. And while he's happy to see Tom or Matt, you can see the disappointment in his eyes. We all know that it's you he wants to see walk through that door.

I'm sorry, I don't mean to make ya feel bad. I just want ya to know that we all feel your absence.

I suppose I should close now so that when Tom shows up tomorrow he can take this to the post office. Rayne, I love you with all my heart. Please know I can't wait to be in your arms again and for us all to be a family once more. We miss you and are here waitin for ya.

All my love,
Lisbet

Jane cleared her throat. While she had told Maddie a few minutes ago that she shouldn't worry about whoever Rayne had waiting for her, she now realized that wasn't true. Clearly, whoever this woman was, she loved the deputy, and there was a good reason for them to be separated for the time being.

"Maddie, I know I said that you had nothin' to worry about, but I think maybe ya should leave things alone. Whoever this woman is, it's clear that the life the deputy left back wherever she came from is waiting for her and a good one at that." She folded the letter and handed it back to the redhead.

"If it's so good, why ain't she here with her? I'll make Rayne forget all about that family life she left behind. And don't you go thinkin' ya can just open your mouth. Ya hear? No one is to know I got this here letter," Maddie took a threatening step towards the other woman.

"Maddie, come on, how you can do—"

"Jane, I swear, if ya say one word about this, I'll kill ya. I aim to have my happy endin' with the deputy, and ain't no one gonna stand in my way. Especially you." Maddie had fire in her eyes. "As far as you know, Rayne got this here letter and told me to burn it. You were there and heard her. Said she wanted nothing to remind her of her past, that her future was here with me. You got that, missy?"

Jane knew better than to cross Maddie, for she had witnessed what happened to one girl that stupidly went after a man Maddie wanted. The pain the girl had suffered and the awful scar that would forever remind her were something Jane didn't want to experience.

"I ain't gonna say anythin', but you're wrong in what you're wantin' to do. But yeah, I heard ya," Jane made a quick retreat to the door. She made her way back to the saloon but could still hear the sound of Maddie's laughter echoing behind her.

Rayne opened her eyes, looked around the room, and found herself alone. She debated on staying put and waiting for someone to come back or just getting up and getting her own drink of water. It didn't take her long to decide. She was thirsty, and she didn't want to wait. She slowly sat up and swung her legs over the side of the bed. She had managed a few steps when the dizziness became too much for her to handle. She was swaying and on the verge of collapsing when the door opened.

Maddie rushed in and soon had her arms around Rayne as she helped her back to bed. "Just what in tarnation did you think you were doin'?"

Rayne's head throbbed as did her shoulder, but she was tired of being in bed, of having to have someone take care of her. She wanted movement; she needed to feel self-reliant again. "I needed a drink and no one was around, so I figured I'd fetch it myself."

Maddie helped Rayne back into bed. "I see, and how well did that work out for ya?"

Rayne took deep gulps of air in an effort to quell the waves of nausea she was feeling. Her fingers clenched around the sheets, as she licked her dry lips. "I just needed a drink of water."

"Well, since you're as pale as a ghost, I'm gonna say you just ain't healed enough. Come on, lay back and I'll get you that glass of water."

Rayne laid her head against the pillow and with a weak low voice said, "Thank you, darlin', I'd be much obliged if ya got the doc as well."

Maddie paused for a second, not at all sure she heard correctly. With a smile, she simply replied, "Of course I will, honey. You promise you'll stay put while I'm out?"

Rayne took a sip from the glass that Maddie held up to her lips before weakly laying her head against the pillow again. Her eyes closed tightly against the pounding in her head. "I ain't goin' nowhere."

It wasn't long before Maddie returned with the doc, who looked Rayne over.

"Well, the good news is the gunshot wound didn't break open again. In fact, it's lookin' pretty damned good. Rayne, tell me, has the pain in your head eased up at all?"

"No. In fact, I'd greatly appreciate it if you'd put me outta my misery, and I don't rightly care how ya do it."

"Now, Rayne, you don't mean that," Maddie injected.

Rayne didn't open her eyes but did manage to growl her response.

Doc Granger reached into his black medical bag and pulled out a brown bottle. "Rayne, I want ya to take a drink of this here medicine. It'll help with the pain. Take it when ya need it ya understand?"

Rayne once again growled but took the medicine.

Satisfied that he'd done all he could do for his patient, Doc stood up and motioned for Maddie to follow him. Once out in the hall, he spoke, "Now the gunshot is healing nicely, but I'm concerned about the head wound. Have her take a swig from that there bottle a couple a times a day. The laudanum should help with the pain."

"I surely will, Doc, and thank you," Maddie smiled. "Oh, has the sheriff said anything? Do they know what happened?"

"He sent a posse out to ol' Horace's place. They found him dead, a bunch of tracks in the dirt but not much they could use to track the other fella. They didn't even bother to just rob him they flat out just killed him. Hawks says it ain't likely they'll catch 'em, but he's wirin' the other towns around here lettin' 'em know about the killin'. I tell ya, I'm plum proud that Mathews there got off a shot and at least got one of them robbers. Old Horace, he ain't done nothin' bad to no one. Hell, his only crime was blabbin' to the wrong people."

Maddie nodded in agreement. She shook her head as if to rid herself of her thoughts before she made a fool of herself and cried. She cleared her throat. "Well, I should go check on Rayne. I'll make sure she takes the medicine too. Thank you again, Doc."

"Not a problem. Now, you come get me if ya need, alright?"

Maddie nodded and walked back to her room, where she found Rayne sound asleep. Quietly, she walked up to the side of the bed and gently pulled a blanket up over the sleeping woman. She then walked to the chair next to the table and picked up the garment she had been mending.

Chapter Eight

Harry was in the parlor browsing the town's paper, when he heard the sound of the slamming door and rushed to the foyer. When he saw Etta, he asked, "What in the name of God is goin' on that ya gotta be slammin' the damn door?"

"That woman..." Etta flustered, "that woman is nothing but a conniving whore."

Harry tossed the paper on the small table that stood against the wall and calmly walked towards Etta. "Now, darlin', is that anyway for you to speak?" He wrapped his arms around her and pulled her into a hug. He didn't let go until he felt her begin to relax. "Now come on into the parlor. We'll have us a drink, and you can tell me what it is that's got you all riled up."

Etta took a deep breath and let it go slowly. She brought her hand up and smoothed her hair, which sat on the top of her head in a neat bun, then smiled. "I'm sorry for slamming the door like that. Can you forgive me?"

Harry smiled. "Darlin', there ain't nothin' I wouldn't forgive." He tenderly brushed her cheek with his thumb. "Besides, I happen to believe you are quite fetchin' when you're angered."

Etta visibly bristled at the comment and again started yelling. "Fetchin'? You think I'm fetchin', do you? Well, let me tell you something, since I'm so fetchin', you should go see Hawks and discuss how fetchin' I am, right along with how I'm bein' over protective of Rayne and how poor, sweet Maddie is only doin' her Christian duty by nursin' Rayne back to health." Etta grabbed a vase from the table and threw it against the wall where it shattered and fell to the floor in pieces.

Harry, who had been backing up, stopped moving and stood as if stuck to the floor. Etta shouted, "Go! I mean it." She stormed upstairs to her room, where she once again slammed the door.

Harry finally moved and reached for his hat, figuring it was safer if he just went to the saloon. He honestly hadn't meant to upset Etta; he did think she was beautiful when she was angry. Well, not when she was angry at him but others, yes. "Hmm maybe I should talk to Hawks and the doc, see what they really think of Maddie's sudden carin' streak." With his mind made up, he walked to Sheriff Hawks's office. *Maybe I should try to see things from Etta's point of view. Does she see something that I don't?*

†

Hawks looked up as Harry walked into the office. He sat back in his chair and propped his feet up on the desk with his fingers laced behind his head. "Well howdy, Harry, are

78

ya lost? You're kinda in the wrong building, don'tcha think?" he joked.

"Ah hell, Hawks, this here visit falls under the crap we do to keep the womenfolk happy." Harry walked around the office glancing at the wanted posters, stopping now and then to take a good look. He stopped to examine one, took his hat off, and scratched his head. He turned towards Hawks. "Almost looks like him. His eyes are wrong. Butch's are a tad farther apart and a little harsher, ya know? Meaner, I guess you'd say. And that one," he said, pointing to another poster. "That supposed to be me?"

"Well yeah, I suppose so, but unless you're tellin' me that you're the Sundance Kid, I reckon it's just some guy that resembles you. That ain't why you're here is it, to tell me that you're this outlaw? That ain't the reason for this visit, is it?" Hawks laughed.

"I don't believe that's why I'm here. Though I do have to say, that there Sundance Kid, he's one damned good lookin' fella." Harry let out a hearty laugh and Hawks joined him.

"Pull up a chair tell me what brought ya here. It'd be my guess though that Etta told ya about our little visit."

"Yup. Whatever ya told her really put a bee in her bonnet. She came home slammin' doors, and hell, she even threw a vase at me. What in tarnation did you say to her?" Harry sat in a chair in front of the sheriff's desk.

"Ah hell, Harry, I just told her she was lookin' for trouble where there was none. Hell, she came in here a squackin' about how Maddie wasn't lettin' her see Rayne. She said somethin' about havin' a letter for Mathews and Maddie flat out tellin' her to leave." Hawks sat forward and reached for his coffee.

"Yeah, she came in a jawin' about Maddie bein' a connivin' whore. I got the feelin' that she don't believe Maddie is the carin' type. Hawks, you don't suppose she sees somethin' you and I don't?"

"Hell, Harry, I don't know. If ya ask me, she's just jealous that someone else is takin' her place in Rayne's life. It's just Etta bein' jealous is all."

Harry let his head fall. "Lord, please tell me ya didn't tell Etta you thought she was just jealous of Maddie."

"Is my head still attached to my body? Hell no, I didn't mention that to her. But you got a better answer?"

✝

Rayne opened her eyes to the soft glow coming from the lantern that sat on the table. She was actually happy to say that her headache was more like a few hundred sledge hammers pounding on her skull rather than the million from earlier. Still, she took her time and slowly moved up to a sitting position.

It was the squeaking of the bedsprings that brought Maddie's eyes up from her sewing. "How are you feeling?"

Rayne, who was focused on moving, stopped and gave it some thought before answering, "Well honestly, I don't feel a million hammers a goin' at my skull. So I suppose that's good. Something smells real good." She sniffed at the air again. "Is that chicken soup I'm smellin'?" She stretched, forgetting about the wound in her shoulder until her muscle screamed.

"Ooh honey, are you alright?" Maddie quickly stood and rushed to the side of the bed.

"Son of a bitch, I forgot about that," Rayne replied through clenched teeth. After a couple of deep breaths she continued, "So is that soup and fresh bread I smell?"

"Yes, I sent Emily to the dining room over at the hotel for something. I figured you might be hungry—if only for a couple of bites. Do you think maybe you would like to try?"

Rayne licked her lips; she couldn't remember when she'd eaten last. "Hell yeah, I think I could eat a horse."

Maddie smiled, and she reached out and ran her hand over Rayne's arm, pausing over the flexed muscle of Rayne's bicep. "Good, I'll bring you a bowl."

"Don't forget the bread," Rayne chimed in quickly.

Rayne was certain that she had not had anything as good as the soup and bread since, well she really could not remember when. With the pain in her head, she had had a hard time keeping anything other than liquids down.

Something was nagging at her, a feeling that she was missing something important, but for the life of her, she couldn't remember what it was. She had questions she wanted answers to but didn't know who she could trust. The thoughts in her head must have been visible on her face, because Maddie asked, "Honey, what's the matter?"

"Hm, what?"

"You have a frown on your face so somethin' is botherin' ya. Wanna tell me what it is?"

"Nothin' really, I was just tryin' to remember when it was that I enjoyed a meal so much." Her head was starting to pound harder; she was thinking too much. Maybe she should close her eyes. "Supper was delicious, thank you, but if ya don't mind, I'm gonna close my eyes again. Them hammers poundin' in my head are back."

"Oh yes, of course, I should have thought about that. I'm sure you're tired. You're still healin'. Let me take this." Maddie took the bed tray and set it on the table. She turned back towards Rayne, with her hands on her hips. "Do you need some more medicine? I have the bottle right here."

"No, I think if I close my eyes I'll be fine, but thank you." Rayne scooted down on the bed and closed her eyes.

†

Harry and the sheriff were at the bar drinking and laughing at the stories they were telling each other, when Maddie appeared downstairs with the tray in hand. Hawks nudged Harry when he saw the redhead. Harry rushed to grab the tray from her. "Here, let me take that, Maddie. There ain't no need for you to have to carry that."

"Well thank you, Harry. How have ya been? I'm surprised to see ya here. I mean, you've been gone for a while, and I know Etta has missed ya. I figured she'd keep you busy, now that Rayne ain't always under foot. I mean, I just cain't imagine how ya'll got any time alone with her livin' with ya," she said snidely.

"Well now, Maddie, Etta does keep me busy enough. But if I wanna have a drink with my friends, she ain't gonna say nothing. Speakin' about Rayne, how is she doin'? I understand that Etta stopped by earlier to see her friend."

"She did stop by. Unfortunately, Rayne was nappin'. Not that it would have mattered, since Rayne asked me to keep Etta away." Maddie shrugged as she looked at a fingernail on her right hand. "Did little miss holier than thou tell ya that it was me?"

"Miz Maddie, there ain't no need for talkin' about Miz Etta like that," Hawks said, as his eyes shifted to the man beside him. For all the carousing that Harry did, he adored Etta. No one spoke ill of her. Hawks wasn't entirely sure what Harry would do to Maddie should he decide she'd spoken out of line.

Harry's eyes narrowed and grew cold, as he heard Maddie's comment about Etta. Maybe Etta was right about the redhead. "Miz Etta would never say such a thing. She just mentioned that she wasn't able to see her is all. How about I buy ya a drink? I'm sure with takin' care of the wounded deputy and all ya ain't had much time for your usual activities."

Maddie smiled and immediately took Harry's arm. "Why Harry, that be so true, and a drink would certainly be a welcome distraction, especially with such an attractive man as yourself. Thank you." Maddie turned to look at Hawks. "See there, Sheriff, that's how ya treat a lady. You should take a lesson from Harry here." She turned back to Harry with a giggle. "It's too bad I got an injured deputy in my room. Otherwise, I'd show you a real good time."

Harry smiled, though it didn't reach his eyes. "It's just not meant to be, I suppose. One drink and then ya got a patient that needs lookin' after. Jonas, how's about ya pour us a couple of drinks?" Harry noticed the man behind the bar was staring at the redhead angrily.

†

Even through the pain of her headache, Rayne was able to sleep. Her dreams centered on a ranch she didn't recognize, but instinctively, she knew it offered comfort and was important to her. She dreamt of a sweet, raven-haired boy with blue eyes that reminded her of herself, and a feisty green-eyed blonde whose smile warmed her heart and lit up her world. At least in her dream world. Rayne still felt she was missing something but couldn't for the life of her recall who these people were.

In her sleeping state, she tried searching her memory but just wasn't able to grasp their names or why they mattered to her. The only real thing she knew was that she felt an unconditional love from these people and the harder she tried to remember them, the more her head hurt.

At some point in the middle of the night, she awoke. Her head and pillowcase were wet with sweat, and the blinding headache was back in force. It was Maddie's soft whispers and coaxing that had her sitting up long enough to take the offered medicine.

"Shh, it's alright, honey. I know you're in pain. Here, drink this. It'll help soon enough. Lord, your pillow is drenched." She pushed back at the dark hair.

"I'm sorry, I didn't mean…"

"Oh, darlin', don't you worry about that." Maddie reached for a dry cloth and tenderly began drying Rayne's forehead and hair. "I'll fetch another pillowcase. It'll be alright."

A few hours later, Rayne rolled over to the soft, warm body of a woman. In her drug-induced haze, she snuggled into the body. The next time Rayne opened her eyes, the beginning of the morning light was barely making its way over the horizon. She sighed and realized that aside from a dry mouth and slight twinge in her shoulder, she felt good. Her head wasn't pounding, and she had a moment of thankfulness at the lack of pain. As her eyes adjusted, she took a moment to appreciate the warmth of the body next to her and the scent and feel of the red hair that tickled her nose.

Maddie rolled over in Rayne's arm and placed her hand on Rayne's well-toned stomach. Slowly, Maddie moved her hand and trailed her fingers up towards Rayne's ribs, stopping at her breastbone.

Rayne brought her hand up and placed it over the creamy wandering hand. Without provocation, her heart beat a little harder.

Maddie's eyes looked up towards Rayne's when her hand was covered by the other. She felt the strong, steady heartbeat beneath her hand. Rayne's eyes held a mixture of fear and excitement. As Maddie looked directly into Rayne's darkening blue eyes, she set aside her own fear and followed her desire. She placed a series of kisses along the solid shoulder up to the collar bone, then up the neck, teasing the dark-haired woman. Stopping at the neck, her tongue flicked at the pulse point, and she smiled as she heard the tiny catch in Rayne's breathing. Her kisses continued along the column of the neck, stopping now and then to taste and nip at the skin beneath her lips.

Soon, Rayne's fingers wrapped in her hair and guided Maddie's mouth to hers. Kisses that started soft and sweet became fiery and demanding, and soon Maddie's knowledgeable hands were caressing Rayne's body, working their magic. Only when Rayne begged her to stop did they both fall asleep.

†

Harry walked into the house after having a few drinks at the saloon with Sheriff Clinton Hawks. The irony didn't escape him. The pure and simple truth was that he enjoyed the sheriff's company and considered him a good friend. A man like himself had few friends. They ended up one of three ways—dead, behind bars, or on the run when the posse got to close.

Harry stumbled as he made his way from the foyer, caught himself with his arm on the wall, and chuckled as he thought about the life he led. He rode and robbed banks with Butch Cassidy and the Wild Bunch; he'd married Etta, a woman who understood him and he had a great time with. He was friends with a man that could, at the drop of a hat, have him behind bars, yet had plans to play poker with him the next evening down at the saloon.

"Oh hell, I gotta tell Etta what I heard at the saloon from the fellas," he hollered from the bottom of the staircase. He looked up the stairs and hollered louder, "Etta, woman, ain't you curious about what I found out?"

With his balance impaired, he swayed and caught himself against the wall again.

Etta appeared at the top of the staircase; her robe tied tightly around her waist and hands firmly on her hips.

"I guess I don't have to ask where you been." She angrily brought her arms up from her hips and crossed them in front of her.

Harry looked up and saw the woman he loved and broke into a lopsided smile. "There ya are, darlin'. I was just down at the saloon, and woman, I gotta tell ya, I missed ya somethin' fierce." He started up the stairs, each step unsteady. Once or twice, his arms flailed as he almost toppled backward, causing Etta to gasp. As he reached the landing, he flashed what he considered to be a damn charming smile. He wrapped his arms around Etta's waist and pulled her into him. "Darlin' you take my breath away. The girls over at the saloon ain't nothin' compared to you. How's about you give me a kiss," he leaned in for that kiss.

Etta threw her hands up and pushed at his chest, as she turned away from the kiss.

"What's wrong, darlin'?"

"You leave to have a talk with Hawks about Maddie, and you come back drunk as a skunk, wantin' lovin'? I don't think so."

"Hell, darlin', it was only a few drinks." Harry tried to look repentant.

"A few drinks and yet you're stumblin' all over the place. Lord, what would ya be like if you was drunk then?"

"Oh, I don't know…less charmin'?"

"Uh huh, well, you're so charmin' right now that I can't stand much more of it. You're sleepin' in one of the other rooms."

"Aw come on, darlin', don't be like that. I want some company in bed."

"Hm, too bad Maddie is already busy doin' her Christian duty and tendin' to Rayne. Otherwise, I'm sure she would find you as charmin' as you seem to believe you are and wouldn't mind keepin' ya company." The sarcasm was very clear in her voice.

"Hey that was uncalled for, don't ya think? I mean, darlin', for all you know, Maddie is bein' a sweetheart and ain't lookin' for nothin' more than to do a kindness." Harry smirked as he wiggled his eyebrows.

Etta sucked in an angry breath and glared at her drunk husband. "You know your way around this house; I suggest you find yourself a bed and sleep it off," she said in a low, angry voice. She turned in a huff and stormed back to her room, where she slammed the door and turned the key in the lock.

Once behind the door, she let out an angry, "Ugh." The crash told Harry she'd, once again, picked up the nearest object and slammed it against the wall. "Jesus Christ, woman, will you stop breakin' things against our walls? You're not only makin' a mess, but you're makin' it impossible for a drunk to pass out."

†

The next morning, Etta was up early making breakfast. She had coffee, bacon and eggs, the whole spread. In part to make Harry feel miserable, but also hoping to apologize for her behavior the night before. Just because he came home drunk didn't mean she had to throw a temper tantrum, and that's what she felt she had done.

Upstairs, the scents of freshly brewed coffee and cooking bacon reached Harry. Despite a pounding headache and slightly queasy stomach, he had to admit that he was hungry. That might be aided by the fact that he hadn't eaten supper the night before. With his mouth dry, he sat up and swung his legs over the edge of the bed. "God, I hate cotton mouth." He rolled his head to ease the crick in his neck that he'd gotten from sleeping on the pillow wrong, then stood up and stretched. As he scratched his head, he wondered how mad Etta was. Judging from the smells coming from the kitchen, he assumed she wasn't that upset. "Well shit, might as well go face the music."

Harry made his way into the kitchen, scratching his chin. "Somethin' smells good. Ya got the coffee ready?" He groggily made his way to the table.

"You feelin' alright?" Etta picked up the coffee pot and walked towards the table.

"Yup, maybe just a touch of a headache, nothin' serious."

"I guess I was a little hard on ya when ya came in. I'm sorry, I...I was just in a horrible mood, and I shouldn't have taken it out on you."

"I don't suppose I made it any better. I'm sorry for that, darlin'. I reckon I gave you the impression that I thought you was behavin' like a jealous female. I just wanna make sure ya know I don't think that at all."

"Oh, I know you don't think that. I was just mad 'cause I know that's what Sheriff Hawks thinks."

"Yeah, I suppose he does have that kinda impression, but darlin', that's an impression he has about all women. We did have a conversation, though, and went over to the saloon."

Etta, who had just walked back to the table after putting the coffee pot back on the stove, tilted her head slightly and replied in a sarcastic tone, "Really, I never woulda thought that. I mean, what with you comin' home drunk and all."

"It's a saloon Etta. You know better than anyone, men drink in a saloon, and they talk freely when they drink."

"Oh, I know that. I just wasn't in the mood to have you gone most of the night. Did you see Rayne? How is she? Did you talk her into seeing me?"

"Whoa there, darlin'," Harry spoke, as he put his hands up and pushed back in his chair. The smile on his face was teasing. "Maddie said that Rayne was sleepin', so I didn't see her. But, Maddie did tell me that she is startin' to do better."

Etta rolled her eyes. "And it didn't occur to you that Maddie was just tellin' you she was asleep to keep you from seein' her?"

Harry frowned. "I…well, now that you mention it, I suppose so, but now listen. Remember I was tellin' ya how men talk when there's drinkin' goin' on?"

Etta nodded and paused.

"Anyway, you might be right about Maddie. Some of the fellas were tellin' me that she was always lookin' for ways to be closer to her. Seems to me, if a chance to nurse the good deputy back to health arose, Maddie would jump at that, and she did."

"I was right. I knew it!"

"Yeah, now what are ya gonna do?"

"That is the question, isn't it?" Etta tapped her fingertip on the table.

†

It was a surprise that she realized she didn't have much of a headache, and she was able to move her shoulder with a little less pain than she had experienced. It was then that it dawned on her that she wasn't alone in the bed. Vague memories began to flow back to her, and for once in what felt like forever, Rayne felt normal.

Chapter Nine

The days between letters from Rayne had stretched into months. Soon it was springtime again, and Lisbet had grown both tired and frustrated. So much so that she packed herself and Ben, wired Eunice, and caught the train to Colorado, specifically Telluride, Colorado.

It was late when the train arrived, and two tired passengers made their way from the train depot to a house they were told belonged to their friend, Etta. Lisbet, who carried the sleeping toddler in her arms, was grateful that the kind conductor had told her he would send her bags first thing in the morning. She made her way up the steps of the large house and knocked at the door.

Etta paced the floor as she waited for her guest to arrive. When the knock at the door came, she was already reaching for the doorknob. "Oh my, you have your arms full, don't you?" She smiled as she stepped back to let Lisbet in.

"Harry, come take Ben, please. He has to be heavy. Put him upstairs in the blue room," she said, as Harry approached.

"Yup," Harry stated, as he walked up to Etta. "Ma'am." He nodded at Lisbet and reached for the little boy. "Come on, little man, let's get you to bed."

"Thank you," Lisbet replied, as Harry took her son.

Etta smiled as Harry took the boy. Once Ben was out of Lisbet's arms, Etta pulled her into a tight hug. "It is so good to see you, Lisbet."

"I can't even begin to tell you how good it is to see you too. Where's Rayne?" Lisbet looked behind the woman towards the staircase.

Etta paused. "She isn't staying here anymore. She has a room at the hotel. I thought she told you."

"Oh, well I suppose, it's possible that the letters and I simply crossed each other." A huge sense of disappointment washed over Lisbet. She had wanted nothing but to see Rayne and spend the night in the woman's arms. "I suppose it's too late to go see her?"

Etta wrapped her arms around her friend. "Tomorrow will be soon enough. Besides, you'll wanna be fresh and well rested when ya see her." Just then, Lisbet heard Harry's boots on the stairs. "Harry, this here is Lisbet. She is Rayne's wife and my dear friend, and I might say, a mighty fine cook! Lisbet, this is Harry, my husband."

Harry walked towards the two women. As he stopped beside Etta, he reached for Lisbet's hand and brought it to his lips. "Mighty nice to meet ya. I wanna thank ya for watchin' out for Etta while she was out travelin' over your way. I told her I didn't want her making her way here on horseback. It just ain't safe. But she don't listen ta no one. I'm surprised you and Rayne were able to get her to listen to some sense."

Lisbet smiled tiredly. "Yes, well, it worked to our advantage. I was pleased that Rayne had a friend and a place to stay once here. I have to admit that I was worried about her being here alone while she worked to set up the new homestead."

"I'm sorry, I have some dinner set aside for you in the oven. I didn't know how late you'd be or if you'd be hungry," Etta spoke quickly.

"I'm starving and afraid my face would end up in my plate."

"Come on. I'll get it for you; you have to at least try to eat something. How about some coffee?" Etta spoke in a motherly tone, as she led her friend to the kitchen. Harry followed with his hands in his pants pockets.

Etta and Lisbet caught up with each other's lives and how big Ben had gotten, and Lisbet and Harry got to know each other a bit better while Lisbet ate. It wasn't long, however, before Etta's motherly instinct kicked in and she hushed Harry. "That's enough. Lisbet here has had a long few days. Can't you see she's about to fall asleep right there? You head on up to bed. We can talk more tomorrow, Lisbet. Harry, show her to her room while I take care of these dishes, will ya?"

"Oh, let me help you," Lisbet began only to be hushed. Harry chuckled, as he scooted his chair back, waiting for the ensuing argument from Etta to end, then led their guest up to her room.

†

Lisbet woke before the sun was even up and quickly got dressed. She was too eager to see Rayne to wait. After the short walk to town, she inquired as to where she could find Rayne and soon she was standing at Rayne's hotel room door.

She knocked and turned the knob. Her heart dropped to the pit of her stomach, as she saw the love of her life pulling on her jeans. Rayne's shirt hung open, and behind her, stretched out on the bed, was a redhead who looked flushed and out of breath.

"I'm sorry…I shouldn't have come." She tried to muster some dignity and hide her pain from her voice.

†

The couple had been lying in bed catching their breath when the knock on the door sounded. With a groan, Maddie pouted, "No don't, whoever it is will leave if ya don't answer."

"I got to. It could be the sheriff needin' me." Rayne swung her legs over the edge of the bed, reaching for her shirt which she tossed on. She was pulling her jeans up when the door opened.

†

"Lisbet…" Rayne instantly knew who the woman was and realized she was the woman that occupied her dreams. She knew, instinctively, that she had just messed up her life and that of the beautiful blonde who stood in front of her.

"Rayne baby, who is that?" Maddie called from the bed.

94

Instantly, anger welled up inside Rayne. "Shut up," she hollered over her shoulder at the redhead.

Lisbet was shaking as she turned away. "No, Lisbet, don't go, please…" Rayne called to the retreating woman.

"Oh, let her go and come back to bed." Maddie patted the bed next to her.

Rayne turned and stared at the woman in the bed, her eyes flashing anger. "Get out," she said through clenched teeth.

"What did I do? Come on baby; I'll make you feel better." Maddie propped herself on her elbow.

"I said get out." Rayne walked towards the bed picking up the dress that was on the floor and throwing it on the bed.

"You seriously want me to leave?" Maddie seemed somewhat astonished.

"Now." Rayne pointed to the door.

Maddie got out of bed in a huff. "I don't know what your issue is, but this is very unbecoming of you." She slipped on her dress and stormed out, leaving Rayne standing in the room, feeling sick to her stomach.

†

"She didn't tell you she would be entertainin' women there?" Lisbet asked.

"No…She neglected to mention that." Etta looked at her hands.

"She was pullin' on her shirt; her jeans weren't all the way buttoned. While the redhead stayed in bed, loungin' like she was waitin' for Rayne to get back into bed with her. She even said, 'Baby come on back to bed,' while I was standin'

95

there." Lisbet looked at Etta, her eyes shining with tears. "How could she do this to us?" She lost the battle to keep her tears from falling.

"I don't know. Lisbet, I couldn't go carryin' tales, not knowin' if they was true or not."

Lisbet swallowed hard, as she wiped away the falling tears. "How long..."

Etta closed her eyes, as she heard the question being asked. She smoothed the skirt of her dress, as she sat on the bed next to Lisbet and took the woman's hand. "I suspected. I didn't want to say anything in case I was wrong."

"I asked how long," Lisbet repeated, as anger began to creep into her voice.

"Lisbet, I don't think it really matters..."

"Oh Jesus, just answer my question. How long has it been goin' on?" Lisbet stood and walked towards the window that overlooked a meadow.

"I'm not sure. Sometime after her shootout with the ones that killed Horace, I suppose."

"Rayne was in a shootout?" Lisbet whirled around, her eyes wide in shock.

"You didn't know...oh God. She told me that Rayne had gotten all your letters and that she'd written to you. I assumed Rayne had told you."

"She didn't, so now you get to tell everything you know." Lisbet crossed her arms.

Etta took a deep breath and began, "It was close to six months ago, I suppose. Horace, a local miner, hit a fairly rich vein and was flashin' money and tellin' anyone who would listen about the gold in his mine shaft. During a friendly game of cards, Rayne got the feeling that a couple of boys were up to no good. So she kept an eye on 'em. When Horace left and they followed, well, she followed too.

"When she got to Horace's cabin, she was too late; they'd already killed Horace and were getting ready to ride off. There was a shootout. Rayne managed to kill one immediately, but the other got away and ambushed Rayne. He shot her, and she took a blow to her head on a rock. The bullet went straight through her shoulder, but the doc was pretty worried about the bump on her head. I…I didn't know how bad the injury to her head was. Maddie wouldn't let me see Rayne much." Etta looked at Lisbet. "Maddie took it upon herself to be Rayne's nurse and protector. Lisbet, I tried. I stopped by to see Rayne every day, and there was always some reason that I couldn't go in. I don't trust her any farther than I can throw her. She's pushy and, if ya ask me, a no-good trollop."

Lisbet took a deep breath. "Maybe, but Rayne…still, I found her…them…they clearly had just enjoyed each other. I don't know that I can forgive this." A tear slid down her cheek.

†

Rayne's headache was back full force as she paced her room. Bits and pieces of memories were starting to float back to her. With each piece, she felt sicker to her stomach. She reached for the brown bottle, took a drink and stared out her window as her thoughts whirled. With frustration, she reached for her hat and stormed out of her room.

Rayne found herself at Harry and Etta's door. Without much thought, she pounded on the solid wood.

When the door opened, she found herself face to face with Etta. "I need to see her."

"Don't you think you've caused enough hurt for one day?" Etta stood in the doorway with her arms crossed.

"I ain't sure what I done, but I am sure I need to see her. Now, are ya gonna move?"

"No, I don't think I am…not until you tell me why."

"Etta, darlin', this ain't got nothin' to do with us. Let 'er in," Harry spoke calmly, as he walked up behind his wife.

"No, she is my friend, and I wanna know what…"

"Let 'er in," Harry said with authority, his eyes on Rayne.

Etta looked behind her shoulder at her husband then stepped back. She shook her head and walked away, leaving Rayne and Harry standing there.

"She's upstairs, third door on the left," Harry looked Rayne over. "Seems like a fine woman."

Rayne took her hat off, nodded at Harry, and walked in. She took the steps two at a time. Once at the door to Lisbet's room, she knocked and waited.

Lisbet opened the door. Rayne assumed the red eyes were from crying, as she watched Lisbet step away with her arms wrapped tightly around herself. Lisbet walked deeper into the room.

Rayne closed the door and followed with her hat in her hand. She spoke softly, "I'm sorry…"

Lisbet spun around and responded incredulously, "You're sorry…that's all you have to say? I…" The tears began to fall again, freely. "How could you do this to us?" Pain and anger rang in her voice.

"Look, I cain't tell ya why I got this feelin', but I feel like my entire world just came crashin' down at my feet. I feel I should remember much more than I do, and I don't know why. Can you tell me?" Rayne asked.

"I'm...you're askin' me what exactly?" A frown creased Lisbet's brow, and she shook her head slightly.

"I'm askin' why I feel you're important to me..." Rayne said, lost and confused.

"Oh God, this just keeps gettin' better. Why am I important to you? I'm sorry Rayne, but I don't think this is the time for playin' games."

"I ain't playin' any sorta game," Rayne snapped. "I have been dreamin' of you, and...and a ranch, a little black-haired boy. I know in my heart that we was happy. But I don't remember the boy's name. Hell, I cain't tell ya why I knew yours when ya opened my door, but I did. I know that I feel like I love you and that we was happy. But I don't know that for a fact. I don't remember."

Through sobs and falling tears, Lisbet stood and stared as she seemed to listen to what Rayne was saying. With angry swipes at the falling tears, she said, "Fine. I'm important to you cuz I'm your wife...at least in our hearts and our eyes, we are, or rather were, married. That little boy you say you cain't remember is our son, Ben. Actually, he is your brother's son, but we are raisin' him as ours." She paused and shook her head. "I can't believe I'm actually havin' to tell ya all this. I must be crazy."

"No...No, ya ain't, please don't stop. The ranch, it's ours ain't it?"

"I...I can't do this." Lisbet shook her head and put her hands up as if she were trying to stop something. "I don't believe you right now. Pretendin' you don't know..."

"I didn't...I don't know what happened." Rayne watched the tears fall and knew she was responsible for the hurt Lisbet was feeling. "I…Honestly, I didn't know what I was doing."

"Oh really? Well, let me tell you what you did. You took another woman to bed…"

"That's not what I meant," Rayne said, louder than she had intended, as she walked towards the blonde.

"*Don't!* Don't you dare yell at me, and don't come near me. I wasn't the one that allowed someone else in my bed. I wasn't the one that let all those nights of loneliness get to me…in fact, I wasn't the one that insisted on leaving our home and everything we had for this," Lisbet threw her arms open to encompass their surroundings. "Remember you promised me that you wouldn't forget about Ben and me, about our family. You promised that you'd come back to us. Or was that just a line you used to get what you wanted? Ya tell me that ya don't remember me… us…I don't see how any of this is gonna work. I was a fool to think it could."

"No Lisbet, please. I honestly don't…you said I promised to come back to 'us'. That's you and the boy…our son. Jesus why cain't I remember this?"

"I can't, I can't do this." Lisbet shook her head as she looked at Rayne, disbelief etched on her face.

"I… so we're a couple," Rayne said as she rubbed the back of her neck, "but why would Maddie, why would I be with her."

"You're askin me? I…"

"She said her and I were together. Why…"

"No, I'm not doin this, how can you be standin' here askin' me all this? I need you to go." Lisbet choked back her tears, her hand going up as if to push Rayne away.

"I'm tryin' to understand. I understand I've hurt you, I'm tryin' to figure out how... why this happened." Rayne said as she took a step towards Lisbet."

"Ya wanna know why, because you bedded another woman. That's why, you're standin' there tellin' me you don't remember me, us...and ya want me to tell ya why this is happenin'." Lisbet let out a disbelieving laugh. "I need to get out of here... I, what am I doing?" She walked towards the bedroom door.

"Wait Lisbet, no don't go. I gotta...I can't, please don't leave." Rayne pleaded.

"I can't see you anymore, I don't want to look at you." Lisbet replied in a sad, tearful voice.

"I can make this right," Rayne softly said, even as she felt her heart sink into the pit of her stomach. "Ya gotta forgive me,"

Lisbet stopped in her tracks and looked over her shoulder at the tall, dark-haired woman she couldn't imagine living without, and quietly replied, "You...I don't know that I can forgive you this." Lisbet walked out of her room.

Rayne stood there watching Lisbet walk out the door, unable to move as her own tears started to fall. She didn't know what to do, so she sat on the bed. She honestly didn't remember everything, but she instinctively knew that what Lisbet said was true. All she had to do was look at the blonde, and she knew they had married each other in their own eyes and hearts. She knew that they had been happy, her heart told her that even without having the memories. She stood and walked to the window and looked at the meadow below. The blonde was walking hand in hand with a little boy. Ben. Lisbet had said his name was Ben, and he was their son. How could she have forgotten that?

Harry tapped on the door with his knuckle before entering. "She was mighty upset. Etta is on her way out the door. Looks to me like things are in a mess."

Rayne looked at the man she considered her friend and unconsciously reached into her pocket for the brown bottle. She twisted the lid. "How can I not remember everything?"

"I'd say let's go into the parlor and have a drink, but I'm thinkin' it's best we're not here drinkin' when them two come back in. So let's head to the saloon."

†

The two walked into the saloon and Harry hollered, "Hey Jonas, a bottle of whiskey and two glasses over here," then proceeded to a table in the corner. When a couple of girls walked towards them, he shook his head no, and they found another table to approach.

"So, we ain't had a chance to talk here lately, have we?" He took a seat.

"No, we ain't." Rayne took her seat as well.

"How's the shoulder?" Harry acknowledged Jonas and signaled with his eyes that the man should just head back to work.

"It's better. Let me tell ya, I cain't says I miss the soreness none." Rayne rotated her arm. The one thing she made sure she did was rotate it now and then, otherwise it would get stiff as hell.

"I noticed you're still takin' laudanum."

"Helps with the headaches." Rayne took a shot of the whiskey and watched Harry.

"Yup, I can imagine. Ya know, I remember hearin' that Doc Holiday used it quite a bit. Some said he couldn't make it through the day without his bottle."

"What are you gettin' at Harry?" Rayne felt herself getting defensive.

"Nothin' really. I guess I'm just wonderin' how many bottles ya go through in say a couple of days?"

"I use it, but I ain't dependent on it like Doc." Rayne sat her glass down a little hard.

"How often ya get them headaches? And don't go gettin' your hackles up. I'm just catchin' up with ya is all." Harry reached for the bottle and poured them another shot.

Rayne relaxed. She took her glass and sat back in her chair, as she stared at the amber liquid and thought. "Honestly, seems like I always got one. Sometimes it's worse than others though."

"Yup, I remember once Old Butch and I got into a punchin' match, and I took one to the head. Felt like someone was in my brain with an ax."

"I'll tell ya there's times I wish someone would put me outta my misery." Rayne chuckled.

"I bet Maddie takes good care of ya, though, if ya know what I mean. Ain't nothin' better for a headache than a little lovin'."

Rayne felt a little uncomfortable at the mention of the redhead. So much so that she looked over her shoulder. With a sense of relief, she let out a low sigh when she didn't see her.

"Come on, ya can tell me. I gotta live through you. Etta would kill me if she even thought I was consortin' with that hellfire."

"We're friends, right Harry? I mean if I tell ya this is tween us, it stays tween us, right?" Rayne sat forward and lowered her voice.

"Of course. I may be an outlaw, but I'm a man of my word, and ya got my word."

"Maddie is a little…seems like there's only one thing on her mind. Sorry, make that two things. She's been naggin' me about us movin' into a small house, and it's always right after or right before we, you know. And Jesus, the woman is always rarin' to go."

Harry laughed. "I've heard that about Maddie. What's the matter? Most are happy that she's always willin'."

"Ya gotta talk sometimes, though. Lisbet and I always talked and laughed," Rayne said without thinking.

"Well, hell yes, there's more to life than fuckin'. Etta and I are…well she knows me better than anyone. She knows my moods, ain't nothin' I cain't tell her."

"Exactly. Maddie, she ain't interested in knowin' about my day, or how I'm feelin'."

"You and Maddie, ya'll started kinda quick didn't ya. I mean, one minute you're savin' for a ranch out here, workin' with Hawks, then you're movin' into town and all cozy with Maddie."

"Harry, before I was shot, were you and Etta against Maddie and I bein' together? Maddie said that we was already becomin' a couple, but that you and Etta didn't want us together, so we was keepin' things quiet. That true? Is that the reason ya didn't visit me after I was shot?"

Harry's surprise showed on his face. Rayne quickly spoke again, "I'm sorry, I shouldn't have said anythin'."

"Look, Rayne, I ain't sure what all Maddie was thinkin', nor what you was doin' when you weren't at the house. But I do know when we was together, there was nothin' more important to you than buyin' some land and starting your ranch so you could get Lisbet and your boy here. Hell, you lived and breathed Lisbet and that ranch."

"So, I wasn't courtin' Maddie?" The color drained from Rayne's face.

"Not that I was aware of. Hell, ya went to work and was back after, always at the house or out lookin' at land with me or Hawks."

"I don't feel so good." Rayne paled.

Harry jumped to his feet and reached for Rayne. "Come on let's get some air."

As they were walking towards the door, Maddie approached them. Harry stopped her with his hand before she was able to wrap an arm around Rayne. "Not now, Maddie."

"Why? What's wrong with Rayne? Rayne, honey, you alright?" she asked. When Harry stepped between her and Rayne she spoke louder, "Hey, you can't keep me from Rayne, not when she's sick. It's my job to take care of her."

Harry had almost had enough and was about to speak when, from the corner of his eye, he saw Rayne sort of spin and fall to the ground. He quickly knelt down beside his friend and loosened her vest and the top buttons of her shirt. "Get Doc Granger."

Maddie positioned herself on Rayne's other side and attempted to take over. When Harry reached out his hand and grabbed her arm, their eyes locked. He coldly said in a low voice, "Until I hear differently from Rayne, I suggest you get away from her right now."

"How dare you?" Maddie began to shout, only to stop as Doc Granger appeared.

"Let me see her, Maddie," he said as he approached. "What happened?"

"She was walkin' out with Harry, and she all of a sudden collapsed," Maddie spoke.

"Harry, what happened?" Doc looked at Harry.

Maddie angrily said, "I just told you."

"Maddie, I need to know what was goin' on before she collapsed. Unless you were sittin' or walkin' with em, ya don't really know."

"She was having a bad headache and took some laudanum followed by a shot or two of whiskey. We was talkin' about things, and she all of a sudden said she didn't feel good. I suggested some fresh air, and next thing I know she went down. I loosened her vest and the top buttons of her shirt, hopin' that would help," Harry said in a rush.

"Alright, let's get her to my office, so I can examine her."

"My room's closer," Maddie spoke, as she turned her head to a group of men.

"Boys, help her to my office. I'll be right behind you," Doc ordered.

"But my room is—"

"Maddie, I ain't got time nor patience to argue with you. Let me do my job."

The group entered the doc's office, and he started barking orders at his wife. "Get me a cold cloth. Give her some room boys. Thank you. Harry, ya can stay in the waitin' room if ya'd like. I'll let ya know how she is soon as I can."

†

It was about half an hour later when the doc came back into the outer office. Harry stood as soon as he heard the door open. "How is she?"

"She's awake. Seems she's been takin' more laudanum than we knew, and the whiskey today didn't settle too well with her. I felt like I was walkin' up to a tense minute between you and Maddie. Wanna tell me what that was about?"

"Doc, I ain't much into tellin' other people's business."

"I'm aware of that Harry, but unlike most small-town doctors, my patient's welfare is deeper than just providing some medicine. I ain't into tellin' tales either, if that helps any."

"Let's go into your office," Harry said, as he looked around.

Once behind closed doors, Harry told the doc about Lisbet, Rayne, and Maddie and how Rayne told him what Maddie had told her about their courting.

"Oh Lord, I was afraid Maddie was up to no good." Doc sat back in his chair and drummed his fingers on his desk. "You say that Rayne told you she didn't really remember much about before the shootin'?"

"Yeah, she told me she felt more than she remembered, and when we was talkin' about her relationship with Maddie, she unconsciously compared it to hers and Lisbet's. It was like she didn't even realize she was doin' it."

"Anything else you can think of that might be of help?" Doc sat forward and placed his elbows on his desk.

"Not that I can think of. I ain't really seen much of Rayne since she got shot, and when Etta has seen her, Maddie's been with her and she ain't really talked."

"Alright. And you say that her wife, Lisbet, is in town?"

"Yeah, arrived last night with their boy. Shoot, I suppose I should head home and let both her and Etta know what's happened. She gonna be alright, Doc?" Harry sat forward in his chair getting ready to stand.

"She should be, yes. I'm worried about what appears to be her reliance on the laudanum. If she is addicted, it's gonna be tough for her to shake. Trouble with a wife and woman on the side ain't gonna help none. Especially if one of the women is Maddie. Lord, that woman would make a saint turn to drinkin'." Doc scratched his head. "I'm gonna keep her here tonight and keep an eye on her. With me and the misses around, we can better keep Maddie at a distance, at least for a little bit."

"Alright, Doc, then I'm gonna head back home. If there is anything ya might need, be sure to let me know. I'm gonna see if I can talk Lisbet into comin' to see Rayne."

"That might help, you never know." Doc stood and walked Harry to the door.

†

Etta walked with Lisbet and watched as Ben ran chasing a butterfly. "I just don't understand it; you're sayin' she is claimin' she don't remember you or Ben?"

"That's exactly what she said, although she said she *felt* that we are important to her and that she wouldn't do anything to hurt us."

"Do you believe her?" Etta leaned over and picked a dandelion.

108

"I don't know. The look on her face makes me believe that she believes it, but…I'm so hurt, I don't know that I can believe her."

"Lisbet, I can't tell ya what happened after she was shot. Like I said, Maddie made it impossible for me to see her. But before that she would go to work and come home. When she wasn't workin', she and Harry, and sometimes the sheriff, were looking at land. She was intent on findin' the right piece of property for you and Ben."

"Findin' property ain't gonna happen when she's spendin' time in bed with another woman." Lisbet wiped a tear away.

Lisbet and Etta were still in the meadow when Harry arrived back home. He walked out to tell them about Rayne. Lisbet was still too hurt and angry, and refused to go into town to see Rayne.

†

"Harry, what do you think really happened between Rayne and Maddie?" Etta asked, as she brushed her hair.

"Ya want my honest opinion?" He stretched out on the bed.

"Well, of course."

"I believe Rayne is one confused gal. I don't believe she knew what she was doin'."

"Really, how do you not know you're cheatin' on your wife?"

"Ya don't if ya cain't remember ya got one."

"Please, not you too." Etta slammed her hairbrush down on her vanity and turned to face her husband.

"Etta, Rayne took one hell of a blow to her noggin', it might have scrambled her brain a bit. And honestly, Maddie is a force all on her own."

"You did not just say that to me."

"Say what? You asked my honest opinion." Harry sat up.

"Maddie is a force all on her own...really, does that mean she's entertained you?" Etta stood up and placed her hands on her hips.

"Whoa, hold on there. Ya can't ask my opinion and then be mad when I give it to ya. Have I been to bed with her? No! But come on, ya know I ain't no saint when we ain't together. I ain't, however, stupid enough to bed another woman when we are. All I'm sayin' is, when Maddie gets somethin' in her head she goes after it full force.

"Yes, well she went after my best friend's wife. I don't like it, and I don't like her. She is a manipulative bitch." Etta turned to face the window.

Harry sighed then stood up from his place on the bed and walked towards her. When he stopped behind her, he tenderly reached out and turned her to face him. With his eyes looking deep into hers he softly asked, "Etta, what's really botherin' ya?"

Etta wiped a tear away. "I'm afraid...Harry, you didn't see 'em together back in Willow Springs. I swear, if there was ever two people that loved each other, it was them. What would happen to us if some Maddie decided to set her eyes on you?"

Harry sighed and pulled her tightly against him. "Etta, darlin', that ain't never gonna happen. There ain't a woman out there that compares to you."

110

"But you just said you have other women when we aren't together," Etta replied, as more tears fell.

"It's only for a night's entertainment. It's a roll in the hay nothin' more. This afternoon, Rayne and I was jawin', ya know, before she collapsed. She was tellin' me, and she didn't realize she was even sayin' this, but she's right. She was sayin' there's women ya can talk to and be friends with, who know your moods and care about your day, then there's women like Maddie always ready for fun, but nothin' else. Don't take this wrong, but with you, I got me the best of both worlds. Look, what I'm sayin' is, I love you with all my heart, and there ain't no room in it for anyone else."

"Oh, Harry, don't you see? That's what Rayne told Lisbet before we left the ranch too. And look at where they are."

"Rayne is lost right now, but deep inside she knows where her heart is. She will find her way back. And Lisbet don't know it, but she'll be there waitin' to welcome Rayne back with arms wide open."

"How do you know that?"

†

The next morning, Maddie was at Doc Granger's office bright and early, demanding to see Rayne. "Now, Maddie, I already told ya that Rayne needs her rest."

"She's been restin' all night. I demand to see her. I wanna know what's wrong with her." Maddie's eyes flashed with anger.

Rayne, who had been able to hear the commotion outside her door, got to her feet and reached for the robe that lay at the foot of the bed. She slipped it on and slowly walked to the door and opened it. "Jesus Christ, Maddie, give it a rest. It's okay, Doc; I'll talk to her. Uh, there ain't been anyone else askin' to see me has there?"

"No, not yet. I'm sorry Rayne." Doc glared at Maddie, who merely smiled smugly.

As soon as the doc had turned to walk away, Maddie began, "Who else ya expectin'? That woman that barged in on us yesterday? Who was she? What'd she want with you?"

"It don't concern you, so don't go worryin' about it." Rayne made her way back to the room she had just come out of.

"I'm sorry, but it does concern me. She acted like she had some claim on you. Clearly, she didn't know about us. Who is she Rayne?"

Rayne's head began to pound again, and she rubbed her temples. "I done told ya it don't matter."

"Rayne, I don't believe you're thinkin' clearly. I'm the one that nursed you back to health. I'm the one that's devoted my time to you. We are a couple, and I'll not have you messin' around on me. Ya hear me?" Maddie pushed Rayne's shoulder.

Rayne whipped around, her blue eyes ice cold and her voice even colder. "No, I don't think you are thinkin' clearly. I didn't ask you to nurse me or devote your time to me. You done that all on your own. And do you honestly believe you have any right to talk to me about messin' around on you, let alone talk to me in that tone of voice? Let's get one thing straight here; you're the whore, and you have lied to me from the beginnin'."

Without thinking Maddie reached her hand out and slapped Rayne across the face. "How dare you…"

Rayne's head snapped back, and her hand shot up and grabbed the redhead's wrist. She pulled her close as she growled low and deep. "Do not make the mistake of thinkin' you'll ever do that again. I dare because that's what you are. Did you think I wouldn't find out? Does this ring a bell... 'no one wants us together, Etta, Harry, Hawks, they're all against us?'" Rayne pushed Maddie away from her. "I asked Harry about that, he didn't seem to recall me ever even behavin' like I was courtin' ya. Now, I gotta ask why that is?"

"I'm sorry, I didn't mean to hit you like that. I wasn't thinking. And I told ya that Harry and them don't want us together. Of course, he's gonna tell ya that he'd never have said anything like that. Honey, come on, let's put this behind us. Let's go back to my room. I'll get us some breakfast and take care of ya." Maddie approached Rayne again.

Rayne gave a laugh of disbelief as she backed away. "You really just don't understand do ya? Ya know what, just...my head is throbbing, I'm gonna go back to bed,"

"Rayne, enough of this. Come on, let's get you home and I'll put you in bed." Maddie once again walked towards Rayne.

That's when Rayne shouted, "Leave now!"

Maddie was still walking towards Rayne, when Doc opened the door. His voice made it clear there was no room for Maddie to argue, "It's time for you to go, Maddie. Rayne is my patient, and she needs rest."

Maddie took a breath and, with a huff, turned on her heel. "Fine. I'll be back later this afternoon. Maybe then you'll be in a mood to listen to reason." She passed Doc in the doorway. "Doc, as always, good to see you."

As soon as the woman had left, Rayne collapsed down on the edge of the bed, dropping her head into her hands. The pain was taking its toll on her.

Doc quickly moved to her side. He reached for the water pitcher and poured some in the basin. He soaked a cloth in the cold water and wrung it out. "Rayne, come on, lay back. I know it hurts, this'll help." He applied the cold cloth to Rayne's forehead.

"Just give me some of the medicine, Doc, it helps," Rayne said through a wave of nausea.

"Now, we talked about that last night. I think it's best if we try to work through these headaches without it."

"I agreed when I wasn't hurtin' so damned much. Now, I've changed my mind."

"I'm here ta help ya through this. It'll pass."

Rayne's head eventually began to calm and she fell asleep. Doc sighed, took the washbowl, and left the room.

†

"How is she?" his wife asked, as he walked into the kitchen with the bowl.

She poured him a cup of hot coffee and put a plate of biscuits and jam on the table, as he poured the water out.

"Restin' right now, fortunately, this time she didn't demand laudanum, just suggested it. Don't mean she won't next time. It's gonna get worse before she kicks this."

"That Maddie don't help none, I'm sure. I told ya a long time ago, anyone that got mixed up with that one was in for a long, hard time of it."

"Maddie don't mean no harm." Doc stopped, thought, and amended his words. "Maddie's a handful, that's for sure. She's just lookin' for what we all are."

"Hm, no sir, not that one. That one thinks she is more deservin' than anyone else. You should see her when she's in the mercantile, always lookin' down her nose at things there. Behaves like she's doin' the Olsens a favor by shoppin' there."

Doc sat down and ran his fingers through his hair, his head back as he stretched his neck. "Sounds like Maddie." He sighed, reaching for the hot cup of coffee. "I do know that whatever was goin' on with them two, Rayne is feelin' pretty much like she was tricked into it."

"I gotta say I kinda feel bad for the deputy. Seems too nice to have to deal with that one."

"Yup." Doc smeared jam on a biscuit and took a bite. "Mm hmm, I do believe this here is some of the best jam you've ever made."

Chapter Ten

Rayne shook and shivered through nights of horrible withdrawals, still dealt with the headaches, and of course, Maddie, who wasn't taking Rayne's change in heart too well. Even though Rayne wanted to say the hell with it and demand laudanum, she didn't. She'd lost a good six months of her life and made one gigantic mistake due to her addiction; she was determined to kick it. And with the clearing of the drug, she slowly began to remember things.

She went to work, and she walked the town. Occasionally, she would stop in at the bar for a drink, maybe a hand or two of cards, and she would ride out with Harry and Hawks looking for land. The one thing she hadn't been able to do was get Lisbet to talk to her.

One day, she'd stopped at the bar. The piano was playing a lively tune; she and the boys were playing cards, joking and laughing. Maddie walked up behind Rayne and put her arm over her shoulder. "Hello, darlin', so ya can come play cards but not to see me?" Her voice was tinted with anger and frustration.

Immediately, Rayne's attitude changed, gone were the laughter and the smile. "Boys, I think I'm played out."

"Oh come on, Rayne, ya can't take our money then run and not give us a chance to win it back," one of the boys said loudly.

Rayne had shrugged away Maddie's arm and pushed her chair away from the table. "Sorry fella's, I gotta head back to work." She put her black Stetson on her head and started for the swinging doors. Maddie followed.

Lisbet had been walking towards the mercantile across the street, when Rayne came through the swinging doors. It had been Maddie's loud voice as she hollered Rayne's name that made Lisbet turn in their direction. She looked over just as Rayne caught sight of her. Lisbet went to turn but not before seeing Maddie turn Rayne's face towards her own, placing what appeared to Lisbet as a passionate kiss, smack on Rayne's lips.

Lisbet quickened her pace, and Rayne quickly went after her. Maddie tossed her head back in laughter.

"Lisbet, wait, please," Rayne yelled, as she ran across the street.

Lisbet stopped, gathered as much dignity and grace as she could, closed her eyes, and took a deep breath before she turned. "Rayne, I don't have anything to say to you. I need to get some items for Etta and get back to Ben."

"Can I...I can help you with shoppin', and um, maybe give you a ride back to Etta and Harry's. Maybe see Ben?" Rayne asked.

"No, I don't think that's a good idea, but I suppose it isn't fair of me to keep Ben away from you. If you want, I'll have Etta or Harry bring him into town tomorrow, and you can work somethin' out with them. I don't believe you need me around for that."

"Lisbet, please." Rayne nervously fiddled with her hat.

"Rayne, I don't think there is anything for us to say to each other. I need to go." Lisbet turned back towards the door of the mercantile.

"Lisbet, I—I have things to say. I just need you to listen to me to try to understand."

"Not now. I'm not ready to hear anything you may have to say. Now, please, leave me alone." Lisbet walked away, leaving Rayne standing on the wooden sidewalk.

Rayne put the hat back on her head, turned, and walked towards the hotel.

†

The next morning, there was a knock on her door. When Rayne answered, she was surprised to see Harry and Ben standing on the other side. True to her word, Lisbet had sent Ben for a visit. As soon as the door opened, the excited little boy took one look at her and flew at her. When the little arms wrapped around her legs and she heard the tiny voice excitedly cry "Ma!" all the memories came flooding back to her. She was able to recall the first time she'd laid eyes on Lisbet. She remembered Dobson, her father. She remembered the day her brother showed up, dying of influenza, and finding Ben's mother had already passed away. She remembered losing her brother to death a few hours later. Most of all, she remembered making a home and a family with Lisbet and Ben. She remembered how happy and complete her life was.

118

As she hugged the little boy, tears fell. "Ma, why you cryin'?" His tiny hand reached out to brush at the tears.

"Just because, baby, just because."

Harry cleared his throat and shoved his hands in his pockets. "So um, I'm gonna let you two, uh, catch up. I'll be over at the sheriff's office."

Rayne looked up at him. She saw his discomfort and the lopsided lift of the corner of his mouth. "Thank you, Harry. I don't know what to say other than that."

"Yup, of course. Hey, tiger, I'll see ya in a little while," Harry said to Ben, as he winked and turned to walk down the hallway.

Rayne looked at Ben and smiled as she hugged him again even tighter. Her voice was soft and low in his ear, "I've missed you so much."

"Ma, I see Uliet peas?"

"Aw baby, I wish we could, but remember she is at home with Romeo and Apache. I promise you, once I get us a place here, we'll send for them all. Alright? Maybe we'll even see about getting you your own pony. What d'ya think about that?" She realized that she was remembering things about her life before Telluride.

Ben's face lit up. "I want puppy too!"

"Well, I suppose we should talk to Momma about that. Don't ya think?"

"Ma, tell Momma want puppy. Her will listen you."

Rayne swallowed hard through the lump in her throat, as she prayed that she got the chance to put things right. "We'll see, baby." She cleared her throat and said, "So, what do you say we go for a walk, and you can meet Ranger. Then I'll introduce ya to my boss, Sheriff Hawks."

"Who's Ranger?"

"Well, Ranger is my new horse. He's an Appaloosa, and rumor has it he likes little boys named Ben!"

Ben's eyes grew big and excited. "He know me?"

Rayne threw her head back as she laughed, and she reached for her hat. "Oh yeah, he knows all about ya. And he told me that he is so excited to finally meet ya. So come on, let's go. I bet he's hopin' that ya bring him some carrots or an apple."

Together, they walked down the boardwalk, hand in hand. Rayne told her son about their new town and new friends, and Ben asked questions, just chattering about whatever popped into his head.

On their way back from the stables, Maddie, who had been standing outside the saloon, spotted Rayne. "Rayne, hey darlin'." She hurried across the street to the pair.

Rayne smiled at Ben. "Come on, Ben, let's walk a bit faster ok?"

Unfortunately for Rayne, Maddie caught up to them. Maddie had a big smile on her face as she approached. "Hey there, darlin', if I didn't know better, I'd say you was ignorin' me." She wrapped an arm around Rayne's shoulder and leaned in to kiss her.

Rayne pulled away from the kiss and shot an ice cold look at the woman, who ignored it. "Oh, darlin', you need to relax. I can help ya with that." She smirked, then looked down at the little boy and back at Rayne. "Whose kid ya got taggin' along with ya?"

"He's my son. And I'd appreciate if it ya showed a tad bit of decency."

Maddie laughed. "I'm sorry, I thought I heard ya say he's your son." Her eyes held shock. "You got a kid...and ya never told me." Maddie's displeasure crept into her voice.

"Maddie I suggest ya…" Rayne started when her eyes caught sight of Lisbet walking briskly towards them.

"Rayne Coulter Mathews, I'd appreciate it if you'd keep your…women…away from my son." Lisbet angrily approached them and reached for Ben's hand.

"Women…oh honey, you got it all wrong, I'm the *only* woman that matters here. Now tell me, just who are you?" Maddie laughed loudly.

Lisbet grew red at the words. Rayne could see the effort it took to keep the tears and anger from showing. "Ben, come along." She took her son's hand.

"Lisbet, wait," Rayne said. She got louder as she watched Lisbet continue to walk away. "God dammit, I said wait." She watched Lisbet stop and turned to Maddie and with ice cold words, "You will never speak to my wife like that again. Ya hear me? In fact, you will never approach her, our son, or me again, ever. Mark my words, if ya do, it'll be the last thing ya ever do." Rayne turned to walk towards Lisbet and Ben.

"Darlin'." Maddie reached out to stop Rayne. Rayne spun on her heel, and before she realized it, her hand made contact with Maddie's cheek.

Maddie shrieked, as Rayne walked away towards Lisbet and Ben.

"We need to talk." Rayne walked down the boardwalk with her family. She rubbed her hand.

"Did you really just…" Lisbet asked. She knew Rayne's life story, and she knew that Rayne had done things to survive, but she had never seen Rayne behave like she just had.

121

"I'll not have a whore disrespect you like that," Rayne said through clenched teeth. "I …I'm sorry, but we…"

"Not in front of Ben."

"I know, um …" Rayne replied.

"Ben, what do you say we go see if Harry and Etta want to maybe have a picnic?" Lisbet looked at the little boy with a smile, and then to Rayne. "Care to join us for a late-afternoon picnic if they are agreeable?"

"I'd love that, thank you. Uh, we can stop off at the sheriff's office and talk to Harry. He was gonna play a few hands of cards while he waited for Ben."

"Well, we'll just stop and ask him, then maybe he and Ben will go fetch Etta. Give us a chance to set some ground rules," Lisbet said with a smile, as Ben pulled at her."

"Lisbet, I wanna tell ya…"

"Rayne, not now," Lisbet said gently.

†

Lisbet and Rayne walked along the lakeshore, as Ben, Etta, and Harry played in the meadow.

Rayne bent over and picked a wildflower. She brought it up to her nose and breathed in its sweet scent. With a smile, she offered it to Lisbet.

With a sad smile Lisbet took it, as she recalled the past. As she absently twirled the flower, she spoke, "I…thank you for sayin' what you did to that…woman, I appreciate it. I just don't appreciate you havin' Ben around her or havin' him see you strike her."

"Lisbet, I didn't take Ben to meet her, she saw us— me walkin' down the street and ran after us. And yeah, I reckon I didn't think. I mean, before I really knew what I was doin', my hand made contact with her cheek. I apologize that I let myself react that way." Rayne cast her eyes to the ground, as they walked on.

"I've never seen you like that, you was so... angry."

"She shoulda listened to me and stayed away from Ben and me, and she shouldn't have said anythin' to you, let alone the things she did."

Lisbet stopped walking and looked at Rayne. "What difference did it make what she said, or how she said it? What do you care? I mean you threw everything away that matters to us for her? Why does what she said matter?"

"I didn't know what I was doin'. Look. a while back I was involved in a shootout. I took a bullet to my shoulder which knocked me off my horse. When I hit the ground, I hit my head on a rock. I passed out, and when I came to I was in this room with the doc and Maddie takin' care of me. I couldn't remember anything before livin' here in Telluride. I remembered Etta, Harry, and the folks here in town, my name and job, but nothin' about you or Ben or the ranch back home. I believed her when she said that we had a relationship. I questioned it, but was really messed up with the pain and painkillers. I honestly didn't know what I was doin'."

"What do you expect me to say here, Rayne?" Lisbet wiped at the tears then wrapped her arms around herself.

"I don't know. That you can forgive me, that you can see a way for us to work this out...I? I don't love her. Hell, I don't even like her."

Lisbet raised her hands. "Stop it, Rayne. You aren't makin' it any better. This was a bad idea. What was I thinkin'?" Lisbet put one hand on her hip and pushed at her hair with the other.

"No, this was...Lisbet, please..."

"How? How was this a good idea? You are tellin' me that you've had sex with a woman that you threw us away for, and you don't even like her?"

"I was manipulated, she lied to me."

"And you still bedded her, even knowin' that ya didn't like her? How does that even make sense to you? And how do you expect *me* to look past that?"

Rayne took a few steps closer to Lisbet, who didn't move, and tenderly reached up to wipe the tears away with her thumb. "I wasn't in my right mind. I swear to God, this thing with her...she is the only time I strayed."

Lisbet just cried, her tears falling.

Rayne cautiously wrapped her arms around the blonde and brought her closer. She breathed in the scent of Lisbet's hair and closed her eyes, praying the moment would last.

Lisbet sank into the embrace and allowed her arms to wrap around the tall woman and held tightly.

Chapter Eleven

Clinton Hawks walked into the saloon, stood at the entrance, and glanced around the room. His eyes stopped on a tall, voluptuous blonde. He saw Rebecca Fiore look in his direction. He watched, as with a laugh and a backward toss of her head, she gently slid her hand off the shoulder of the man she had been chatting with and moved away from the bar. With her hand placed on her hip, she walked towards the sheriff, her hips gently swaying from side to side, a true smile growing on her red, kissable lips.

Clinton took his hat off and walked towards the approaching woman. Before he could say anything, he heard Maddie calling him. He turned his head slightly and, as he saw the redhead approaching him, he swore under his breath. "Miz Maddie." She came to a stop directly in front of him. "I was just headin' to the…"

"I know where ya was headin', and Rebecca can just wait a second. I wanna know what the heck is goin' on with Rayne. Just who is that blonde that rode into town thinkin' she got a claim on her?" Maddie's lips tightened.

"Well now, Maddie, I don't rightly know Rayne's business. From what Harry tells me that blonde is her wife, that's what Etta told him. They've come to join her and build their home here."

"I need her to go back to wherever she came from. You know that me and Rayne was gettin' serious. Send her away, Sheriff."

"Miz Maddie…I ain't got cause to send her away. I woulda thought, in your profession, you understood that there is generally a Mrs. at home that he, you know, the man you're screwin', or she in this case, ain't leavin'," Clinton's eyes locked with Rebecca's. "Now, if you'll excuse me, I'm gonna get me a lousy beer."

"Sheriff," Maddie's voice grew shrill with anger.

The sheriff, who had begun to walk away, stopped and turned on his heel. "Maddie, stop it. Ya ain't gonna convince me that whatever it was tween you and Rayne was anything more than distraction. You knew damned well she was already committed elsewhere. Or don't ya remember all them letters ya burned? I know about em, and I know ya had someone read em to ya. So ain't no use cryin' to me about how much ya love her." With that, Hawks once again headed to the bar, Rebecca half a step behind.

Maddie stood there staring at the two as they walked away, her blood boiling. *How dare he talk to me that way?* She spun on her heel and stormed out of the saloon, not caring one bit that she'd left a fella waiting for her.

†

At the bar, Clinton ordered a bottle of whiskey with two glasses, then he and Rebecca headed upstairs to her room. Clinton sat down at the foot of the bed, while Rebecca poured them each a glass.

Clinton sat staring at the floorboards, and Rebecca sat next to him, handed him a glass, and gave a weak smile.

"Clint, you're thinkin' too much. You're worryin' whether I'm confused about my part in this thing that we got goin' on."

Clinton immediately brought his head up. "No...No, of course not. Why would you think...?"

"Clinton, I heard whatcha told Maddie. I know full well the married ones always go home to their wives. I ain't got no illusions about us, honey," Rebecca gently rubbed his back.

"Don't that bother you, though? Darlin', you should want more than this."

"Honey, I made peace with the road my life took a long time ago. I have a roof over my head, food in my stomach, and a place to lay my head."

"You're a sweet gal, though, ya should be at home waitin' for a man to come home to ya."

"Yeah, maybe, but that ain't the way life turned out. I'm here instead, so I gotta make the best of it. Men like you don't leave their wives for a woman like me. I don't know why you come see me, but ya do. And the fact is that I like ya. Hell, I love you. I love you a lot, but like I said, I ain't got no illusions. Ya come see me once or twice a week, and we have a good time. I can live with that."

Clinton took a deep breath and looked at Rebecca with a small smile tugging at his mouth. "Yeah, we do have a good time, don't we? Ya know, she knows about us, Sarah knows. I think, at times, hell, I get the feelin' that she's happy that I see you. Does that make sense?"

"I suppose that makes some sense. Why you think that is?" Rebecca scooted up on the bed and rested against the wall.

Hawks scooted up as well. "Ah hell, I don't know. Maybe she don't think I understand what her day is like, or she don't like that I spend so much time here in town and not with her."

Rebecca laughed. "Most say their wives don't understand 'em. Ya wanna know what I think?"

Hawks turned his head and looked at the woman and chuckled. "What, what do you think in that pretty little head of yours?"

"I think it's a reason men use to excuse the fact that they cain't keep it in their pants. Let me tell ya a secret; most men believe that they cain't be a hundred percent honest with us. Ya'll think that we would think less of ya if ya told us that you get scared once in a while, or that ya hurt. We wouldn't, and we don't. It's nice to know that the one you're with ain't afraid to show tenderness, to cry if ya need."

"Aw hell, is that a fact?"

"Yup, ain't that why we get on so good? You talk to me and tell me things that worry you and that you're afraid of—things you don't tell your wife. Ever wonder about that?"

"You're easy to talk to. You don't judge me."

"There ya go."

"Thank ya for the lesson, now come here." Hawks reached for Rebecca and pulled her to him.

Chapter Twelve

It had been a week or so since Rayne and Lisbet had their picnic, and there had been no other contact between them. Rayne wasn't happy with that, but true to her word, Lisbet didn't keep Ben from her. Rayne was still working hard on kicking the laudanum need. The one good thing she could say was that the headaches were becoming less frequent, a fact Rayne was happy with.

One morning, when Harry dropped Ben off, she asked about Lisbet. "What do you want me to tell ya, Rayne? She's hurt, and she's angry."

"Jesus, I know that. Dammit, how the hell can I make it right if she won't give me a chance?"

"I don't know. Maybe ya finally find that damned ranch you came here lookin' for. Maybe ya move outta town, outta this damned hotel room, and behave like ya want her back."

"What the hell are ya talkin' about, I do want her back. Again, how…"

"I said to behave like it," Harry shouted. "Do ya make it a point to stop by the house to pick Ben up, or take him home? No. Do ya stop to see *her*? Again, no. Maybe just maybe, you doin' some of that would tell her ya want her back."

"Harry. She won't talk to me."

"Have ya tried?" With a trace of disappointment in his voice, he continued, as his eyes looked around the room, "Aw shit, I gotta go. I told Etta I'd pick her up and we'd go for a ride in the country." He put his hat back on before he turned to leave. He stopped just before he turned the knob and looked back at Rayne. "This would be a good time for you to stop by, maybe an impromptu outing as a surprise." He winked, opened the door, and left, leaving Rayne staring at his retreating back.

"Son of a bitch, I think he is on my side. Wouldn't ya say, Ben?"

"Son a bitch," Ben repeated.

"Uh, Ben, don't you dare ever say that in front of your momma. She'll have my hide." Rayne wiped her hand over her face. She looked at Ben then smiled as she processed the idea. "Hey Ben, what do you say about goin' fishin', maybe have a picnic? We can stop by and see if we can talk Momma into joinin' us." The more she thought about the idea, the more she liked it.

"Come on, let's go down to the dinin' room and see if maybe Katie would fry up some chicken for us, some biscuits, and a couple pieces of pie. That sound good to ya?"

"Yeth!" the little boy shouted with excitement.

"Alright then, let's go talk to Katie then get a wagon and head over to Harry and Etta's place and pick Momma up."

†

Lisbet heard the whining of horses and pulled the lace curtain back to look outside just as the wagon pulled up. When she opened the door, she saw Rayne jump down and heard Ben excitedly holler, "Momma go fishin' wiff us? Ma said we have chicken and pie. Mon, let's go peas?"

Rayne had taken her hat off and was fiddling with it. "Um he's a tad excited. I was just thinkin' that it's a nice day, and maybe you'd like to join us for a picnic, maybe do some fishin'."

"I don't know. I don't think it's a good idea. I mean, this is supposed to be your time with Ben."

"Lisbet, ah hell, the truth is, I'd like it if ya joined us. I know Ben would love it, and I ain't sure you've had a chance to see some of the beautiful spots around these parts. In fact, if ya don't mind, I'd like to show ya a piece of property I been lookin' at. What do ya say?"

"I...I...okay. I suppose I can fry up some chicken for us. It'll take a while. Think ya'll would mind waitin'?" She wasn't sure she'd given the right answer. A big part of her was excited and nervous, and she was afraid Rayne wouldn't want to wait.

Rayne smiled, but before she could answer, Lisbet was saying, "I'm sorry, of course, you don't want to wait. I don't know what I was thinkin', you and Ben should go on and enjoy the day."

Rayne felt as if a rug had been pulled out from under her. With confusion, she said, "I don't...don't ya wanna go with us? I mean, we can load up in the wagon and stop on the way through town at the hotel dining room to pick up the basket Katie is fixin' up for us. I…I guess I was just assumin' that you'd say yes, so I asked before we left to hitch up that there wagon if she'd do that."

"You did? I mean, of course, I'd like to go with you. I didn't think…"

"Seems to me that we've been doin' a lot of not thinkin'," Rayne replied with a slight smile, "Come on, let's get goin'."

Lisbet blushed, as she realized that Rayne was right. They had both done a lot of assuming. "Let me get my bonnet. Ben, let's go fishin' with Ma."

The two walked a squealing, excited little boy towards the wagon. With a big smile, Rayne held her arm out to help Lisbet up onto the wagon. They made a quick stop at the hotel dining room and headed out of town.

†

"You know, Willow Springs was beautiful, but I have to say that this place is the most beautiful I've ever seen." Lisbet glanced at Rayne then at the passing scenery.

"Yup. I gotta agree with you, and I can't wait to show you the place I got my eye on. It has a creek runnin' through the property that forms a little lake. It's about a hundred acres, prime land. It's beautiful, almost as beautiful as you," Rayne said softly.

Lisbet blushed, as she glanced at Rayne's tanned face. She looked like she was about to be hung, and Lisbet couldn't help but smile. She unconsciously bit her bottom lip. "Is that a fact?"

Rayne glanced over and a look of relief washed over her face. "Uh…yeah, it is." She flashed the same cocky smile that always made Lisbet's heart skip a beat. Rayne looked up. "Look up at those pines and firs up there on them slopes, standin' so tall and sturdy. I want our ranch to be just as sturdy as them trees. I want our family's roots to run just as deep as them trees'." She cleared her throat. "Hey, Ben, this here lake I'm takin' ya to feeds off a creek that comes right off the river. Now, let me tell ya, last time I was there I caught a fish so big it damned near fed the whole town."

Ben gasped before squealing in excitement. "That big fish! I catch big fish too. Momma be right proud iffin I do!" He looked at Lisbet and continued, "Momma, would ya?"

"Of course I would, honey. Would you be proud of me if I were the one to catch a fish that big?" Lisbet winked at Rayne and smiled.

Ben giggled. "Yup."

"What about Ma? Ya think maybe she would be proud of me?" Lisbet glanced back to Rayne.

Rayne nudged her hat and glanced up at the clouds in the sky. "Hey Ben, look up at that there cloud. What do you see?"

"Duck!"

"I see one big fish!" Lisbet looked up at the sky, too, before she started laughing.

"Oh, ya do, do ya? Yeah, I suppose you could say that one there's a fish…a minnow. I think it looks more like a little minnow to me. But don't worry, darlin', I bet it's a sure sign that you'll catch somethin'."

"Oh, thanks for that vote of confidence." Lisbet laughed.

"Yup, anytime, darlin', ya can always count on me," Rayne teased. "Hey, look over there, Ben. Just this side of the tree line." Rayne pulled the wagon to a stop and pointed off to her right. "Ya see it?"

Off to the right, just before the trees, stood a doe with her fawn, grazing on the sweet grass of the meadow. "I bet just about anything that just behind them trees is the buck."

Lisbet sighed at the sight. "This is just so amazing, Rayne. Thank you for sharing it with us."

"I wanna share everything with you." Rayne reached out and grabbed ahold of Lisbet's hand. When Lisbet pulled back, she let the smaller hand go and grabbed the reins to signal the horses to start moving again. "We're just about there. Do ya remember how I taught ya to look for worms, Ben?"

"Yeah."

"Good. While I tether the wagon and unload the picnic basket, you can start lookin' for some."

"Yes, ma'am." Ben smiled.

†

The small family arrived at a suitable spot, got their blanket and lunch spread out, and before long, Rayne had Ben set up with his line in the water.

"Now, I'll be right over there, so if ya feel a tug on your pole, let me know. Okay?" With a nod from Ben, she turned her attention to Lisbet. "So, let's get your pole ready for that huge fish you're aimin' to catch." The statement caused Ben to giggle.

"Hey now, I am perfectly capable of catching a big fish. He is too much like you, Rayne, I swear."

"I didn't say anything," Rayne said defensively.

"Ya didn't have to," Lisbet said with a sparkle in her eye. "Give me that. I can bait my own hook, thank you very much." When Rayne turned the hook over to her and held out a worm, she crinkled her nose. "Can it stop wigglin', and why does it have to be slimy?" she complained.

Ben giggled again, as he watched Lisbet try to bait her hook. After a few attempts to put the wiggling critter on the hook, Rayne took the hook and poor worm away from Lisbet. "Ben and I wanna get some fishin' done. At the rate you're goin' it'll be winter time before ya get that line in the water."

"Hmm, I could have done that had you given me more time," she complained, as she sat down on the grass near the lake edge.

With a wink, Rayne pushed her hat back and looked up at the sky. "Yup." Rayne looked over to Ben. "Ya doin' alright, tiger?"

Just then, the tip of his pole bent, and he squealed at the tug. "I got one, I got one!"

"Alright son, now give it a yank and set the hook." Rayne hurried to his side. She positioned herself behind him, as she gave him instructions. "Pull up on the pole and pull in your line...there ya go, do it again." With a proud smile she looked towards Lisbet. "Look at him, I think he's caught a big one!"

Lisbet had jumped up as well and was now standing beside her son as he pulled in the fish on his line. "It sure looks like it."

"Keep it up son, you're doin' a fine job. Look at it fight, yup, it's gonna be a big one! There ya go, keep doin' just what you're doin'. Get 'im tired out..."

135

"You're doin' great, Ben," Lisbet exclaimed, her eyes on her son.

"Look, can ya see him tryin' to swim away from the shore? Look, Lisbet. It's a beauty!" Rayne excitedly pointed at the fish that jumped out of the water and splashed back down. "Okay, just a little more." She stepped closer to the water and reached for the line. Once the line was in her hand, Ben dropped the pole and jumped up and down as he shouted with glee.

Rayne brought the fish to the shore and held it up for Ben and Lisbet to look at. The fish turned out to be a six inch smallmouth bass. Not a big fish, but big enough to thrill Ben. "Well alright, Momma, I do believe ya got some competition. Ya still think you're gonna catch the big one?" she teased.

†

By late afternoon, the trio had packed up and were heading back to town. With Ben stretched out asleep on the blankets in the wagon, Lisbet and Rayne were left in silence, lost in their thoughts. Lisbet couldn't help but feel comfortable, she'd just spent the day with her family, with the woman she loved. The image of the redhead lying in bed as she beckoned Rayne flashed in her mind's eye, and she was angry and hurt all over again.

Rayne happened to turn just as Lisbet wiped a tear from her eye, and she softly spoke, "Please, don't. It was a mistake, one I would give anything to have never made. I can't take it back, she doesn't mean anything to me."

"Rayne," Lisbet swallowed hard through the lump in her throat. "I know you would, but honey, you can't. And

I'm not sure right now that I can just forget and forgive. No matter how much I love you."

"Ya know, I can't pretend to imagine how hurt you are. I mean, I know how I would feel, and God help me, I know if I were in your shoes I'd want to kill the other person. You're a better person than me. I…I will do anything and everything to prove to you that this will never happen again. I will never give you a reason to doubt me or mistrust me. I will spend the rest of my life making things right again. Today, today was a good day, proof that we can move forward from this. Please…"

"Rayne, don't…I can only go day by day. I can't promise…"

"I know, I know ya can't," Rayne rushed on. "I just…I'm so very sorry that I did what I did. I need ya to know that I honestly didn't know, it was the laudanum and a lie."

"Rayne, why would you believe her and not Etta?" Lisbet was truly interested in the answer.

Rayne was quiet for a bit and then replied, "After I was shot and dealin' with the head injury, I don't recall Etta bein' around much."

"What do you mean she wasn't around? She's our friend. Why wouldn't she go see you, or even insist that she nurse you to health?"

"I don't know. I just assumed that she didn't wanna help me."

"Oh, Rayne, think about that statement," Lisbet replied with annoyance. "Can you tell me that you honestly see Etta not wanting to care for you?"

"Son of a bitch. That bitch lied to me again," Rayne said as it dawned on her.

"Rayne..." Lisbet paused, as she attempted to sort her thoughts. "Watch your language. Ben absorbs everything you say. Did you ever wonder why Etta wasn't around, and does it really surprise you that that woman lied to you?"

"Maddie said that Etta didn't approve of us, that's why she didn't come see me. I...I was drugged, so I never really questioned it or the fact that I didn't truly recall a relationship with Maddie."

"What do you mean you didn't recall a relationship with her?" Lisbet asked, as their eyes locked.

"Lis, I know this ain't gonna make sense. I can't ever explain how things got physical other than the laudanum, but in every other relationship I've had with a woman...you know I ain't no saint..." she said in an effort to keep Lisbet from feeling as though she was flaunting her past. "There's always been some feelin's, an attraction, ya know? I never took anyone to bed that I didn't care about. With her, it was different. When I wasn't takin' the medicine and I was in my right mind, I didn't find her attractive in any way. I didn't like the way she talked, the things she said, I didn't...I was indifferent to her, ya know? Thinkin' on it now, the headaches were always worse when she was around, so I took more laudanum. I didn't feel when I was takin' it."

"Didn't that tell you anything, Rayne?" a trace of disappointment laced her voice.

"I was addicted to the laudanum, so no, I don't suppose I thought about any of it."

The talking stopped until Ben woke, and then they enjoyed the excitement of the chattering boy as he pointed at trees and clouds and whatever he happened to see.

When Rayne stopped in front of Etta's house, there was a sad smile on her face. She turned to Lisbet. "Thank you for goin' today. I know Ben had a great time. I'm hopin' you did too."

"I did, thank you, Rayne. I know Ben had a lot of fun."

"Maybe we can do it again? Picnic, fish, talk about the future instead of the past..." she finished saying, as she looked at the ground.

Lisbet nodded. "I know Ben would love that."

Rayne looked up. "What about you?"

"Yes...yes, I would love it too."

"Good. Uh, let me get the fish, you and Etta can fix 'em up for supper."

"Ma, stay for supper?" Ben tugged on Rayne's hand.

"Oh Ben, I don't know. I should probably get back to town and see if Sheriff Hawks needs me." Rayne looked up at Lisbet.

"No, I think it's a great idea. I mean, I should have thought of it. After all, you did catch most of the fish," Lisbet said. "I know Etta and Harry would love to see you and would like to thank you for the fish."

It was late when Rayne drove the wagon back to the livery stable and walked to her hotel room.

Chapter Thirteen

Rayne walked to the sheriff's office, whistling as the heels of her boots hit the boardwalk. Memories of the night before floated through her mind. The evening meal had been delicious and the company enjoyable. Dinner with her family was just what she had needed. It did, however, highlight to her just how much she missed Lisbet and Ben. It was with purpose that she decided to change directions and headed to the land office. About thirty minutes later, she walked out with a list in her hands.

She was looking at it when she walked straight into Maddie, whose arms wrapped around her.

"Honey, you don't have to run me over if ya want to see me," Maddie said.

Rayne pushed the woman away from her. "I ain't your honey, and trust me, I don't want to see you."

"Rayne, why you behavin' like this? I know you wanna see me, and I know that woman is keepin' us apart. What I don't know is why you're lettin' her."

"You don't know anything. And 'that woman' is my wife. I told you once that you need to stop talkin' about her. I'm gonna tell ya once more, do not say another word about her. In fact, don't talk to me, period."

Maddie reached out to touch Rayne's cheek. "Darlin', you don't mean that. Come on over to the saloon. I'll get us a bottle, and we can head up to my room. I miss you. Come on, baby. I'll make you feel so good."

Rayne stepped back as she pushed Maddie's hand away. "What do you not understand? I don't want you, I don't want to see you, and I sure as hell don't want you touchin' me ever again."

Maddie laughed, as Rayne turned on her heel and walked away from her. "Oh, darlin' you'll come crawlin' back." The smile dropped from her face. "One way or another, I'll have you back where you belong."

†

Lisbet had left Ben and Etta at the mercantile and was on her way to the sheriff's office when Maddie approached her from across the street. With her arms crossed in front of her, she walked confidently towards Lisbet. "I know why ya don't wanna let her go."

"Pardon me?" Lisbet turned towards the woman who had just spoken. She began walking again when she realized who had spoken to her.

"Rayne. I understand why ya got her on a string. You just need to know that ya ain't gonna get her back."

"You have no idea what you're talking about."

"You think you've won, that Rayne is all yours. But ya know who she spent last night with? It wasn't you, was it?" Maddie laughed.

Lisbet paled, as she swallowed hard. "What Rayne does isn't of any concern to me. Now, if you'll excuse me."

"That's good to know, cuz I plan on seein' her again tonight, and tomorrow night and well, you get the picture right? Oh, by the way, you have a good day." Maddie turned and walked back across the street.

Lisbet held her composure until she turned the corner of a building, then she leaned on the wall. With her tears streaming down her face, and her chest heaving with her sobs, she was unaware of a woman approaching her.

"Darlin', are you alright?" the tall blonde woman asked, as she reached out to touch Lisbet's shoulder.

"Oh yes, yes, I'm fine, I just needed to…"

"Lean against a building and cry. You know, I do that exact thing at least once a week. It always makes me feel better. But I'm gonna have to warn you, this here wall is mine. Now, I'm sure we can come to an arrangement to share it. You know, I could use it on, say Mondays, and you can have it on Fridays. What do you say, will that work for ya, hun?"

Lisbet looked at the blonde-haired woman as though she had lost her mind. "Oh, I uh, don't think I…"

"Now, now, don't you go get all embarrassed. I don't mind sharin', really I don't. I was thinkin' we need to maybe put a chair out here so that we have a place to sit as we cry our hearts out. What do you think?"

"I don't uh…"

"Honey, I'm just teasin' ya. I ain't crazy, really. Just sometimes fun to make people wonder. You, however, are in pain, and I can't say that I like it. Unless I miss my guess, you're Rayne's one and only. I'm Rebecca Fiore."

Lisbet was a little afraid to tell this woman her name, but she realized that the woman was kind, and she had made her smile. "Lisbet Stone Mathews."

"So, I was right, you are the deputy's better half."

"I used to be, yes. These days, I just don't know. I ain't got a clue as to who to believe, Rayne or that woman. Why does she insist on ruining any happiness I might have at the moment?"

"You'd be talkin' about Maddie. Maddie is a real snake in the grass. She is plum mean. Here, let's dry those beautiful eyes of yours and go have some tea. I'm a good listener, and I promise I won't tease anymore. Probably won't tease any less either, come to think of it."

Lisbet couldn't help but smile. For some reason, this woman made her smile and feel at ease. With a nod she allowed Rebecca to lead the way to the dining room.

Once inside the dining room and seated, Lisbet asked, "So how do you know Maddie?"

"I work with her. I suppose I should have told you, I'm what you might call a soiled dove." Rebecca reached for the glass of water that had been placed in front of them when they sat down. "I'm not ashamed of that. We play the hand we're given, right?"

Lisbet looked at the woman seated across from her, and it seemed as if Rebecca sat up straighter, almost daring her to say something about what she had just been told.

"Yes, we do. Would you believe me if I said I understand and don't see you any differently than I do any other lady in town?"

143

Rebecca blinked in surprise at the blonde's reaction. With a tiny sigh, a smile began to pull at the corner of her mouth. "I reckon I believe you. I ain't sure why, but I do. Lisbet, I do believe we are gonna be great friends. I'm sorry Maddie is bein', well, Maddie. Are ya alright?"

"I do believe that woman is set on destroying any little bit of happiness I have."

"What happened, if ya don't mind me askin'?"

"She just reminded me that Rayne spends any extra time she has with her. I'm the one married to Rayne and yet—God, why am I telling you all of this? You're a complete stranger." Lisbet wiped a tear that slid down her cheek.

"Hey now, stop that. I know we just met, but there's a reason God brought us together; and I don't know about you, but I can always use another friend." Rebecca leaned forward.

Lisbet sighed. "I suppose I should tell you the whole story." She waited for the waitress to place their tea on the table and leave before she began again. "Rayne came here to expand our ranch. We own the Rockin M Ranch back in Willow Springs, Wisconsin. She felt we needed to expand west so she came here, and well, folks around here aren't as trustin' as she figured. Anyway, it took longer for her to meet people who were willin' to talk to her, and she ended up takin' a job as the deputy. I imagine you knew that and all about that her gettin' shot?" she questioned, taking the opportunity to take a sip of tea as Rebecca nodded her head. "Rayne claims that she was taken advantage of. That Maddie lied to her about bein' in love, and that while she was drugged with laudanum, they slept together.

"I got tired of waitin' for letters and for Rayne to send for us, so I got us tickets, and Ben and I headed here. I arrived before the letter tellin' her we were on our way. Anyway, I got here and was eager to see her. So, when Etta told me that Rayne had a room in town, I showed up knockin' on her door. Imagine my surprise when I opened the door and found Maddie in her bed."

"Oh my. I can't imagine that was pleasant."

"It broke my heart." Lisbet remembered that day as if it were yesterday. "You know, Rayne had the nerve to come knockin' on the door tellin' me that she 'had this feelin' that I was important to her,' but she couldn't remember why. You tell me, how important would that make you feel?"

Rebecca looked at Lisbet. "Honey, can I tell ya somethin', and you gotta promise to listen to me? Do ya think ya can do that?"

"I don't know, I can try…"

"Now, I been workin' at the saloon a long time. One thing I learned, a long time ago, is to spot a man or woman in love. Now men are men, and they got their needs. Who knows why they cain't just keep to one woman, but they cain't. I've also known Rayne since she got to town. Etta introduced us, but also from the saloon where she'd come and play cards with the fellas. Lisbet you cain't be blind, ya know both men and women turn their heads to look at her when she walks into a room. It's safe to say that most would do just about anything to get her in their bed. Now, hold on there." She watched Lisbet's bottom lip tremble and her hand shake, as she placed the glass of tea back down. "Not ever did I see Rayne pay any attention to them or their attentions. Shoot, the girls that did try always complained that she would behave indifferently to them. Always said that

145

whoever had her heart never needed to worry about her strayin'."

"But she did!" Lisbet cried.

"Darlin', don't put it past Maddie to be underhanded. I watched Maddie for a long time, tryin' to get Rayne's attention, and Rayne always kept her at arm's length."

"Well, she wasn't at arm's length the day I knocked on her door. She was in Rayne's bed, naked."

"Okay, I'll give ya that. I'm also sayin' that if I had to bet on things, my money would go towards believin' Rayne. I know Maddie, and she ain't got no conscience."

"Maybe, but to leave Ben and me after a wonderful day and evening and go straight to her, how could she do that?"

"Honey, right now you only got Maddie tellin' ya that. Ask Rayne where she went after she got back into town. Ask me or any of the girls at the saloon."

Lisbet thought about what Rebecca had just said. "Was she there? At the saloon?" she picked at the corner of her napkin.

"No, darlin'. I never seen Rayne come into the saloon, and I was in the main room the entire night," Rebecca sat back in her seat.

"You didn't leave to…I mean…you didn't…"

Rebecca laughed and said, "No honey, I didn't have any customers last night. Clinton didn't come in, and well, I just wasn't in the mood to entertain anyone else."

"I'm sorry, I didn't know how to ask that…you'd think I didn't understand how it works." Lisbet remembered the girls she had lived with before she met Rayne. She remembered her own mother, who had worked as a prostitute.

"Why on earth would you understand how it works?" Rebecca was surprised at the statement.

"Oh, Rebecca, we all have a past. You of all people should know that. I was just lucky enough to have met Rayne."

"I didn't..." Rebecca began to say, only to be interrupted by none other than the tall, dark-haired deputy.

†

Rayne had walked to the sheriff's office and looked through the newest wanted posters, had a nice chat with Hawks, and asked if he could handle things in town. She was eager to go look at some of the land she had been told about at the land office. When he gave her the okay, she thanked him, grabbed her hat, and walked out whistling. She was walking past the hotel dining room when she happened to glance in and see Lisbet sitting at a table. With curiosity, she walked inside.

"Lisbet, Miz Rebecca." She approached the table.

"Well hello, Deputy, how are you this fine day?" Rebecca asked.

"Oh, I cain't complain. The sun is up, not a cloud in the sky, and no sign of trouble from the men at the saloon. And much to my delight, I get to see Lisbet. Overall, I'd say it's shaped up to be a mighty nice day indeed. How about you?" She flashed a smile at them both.

"Oh, I agree it's a fine day. I was just getting acquainted with Lisbet. I do believe I like her," she finished with a smile directed at Lisbet.

"She is easy to like. Lisbet is very special," Rayne replied, her eyes on Lisbet.

"Well, I do believe I'll leave you two to chat." Rebecca winked at Lisbet, as she stood.

"Rebecca, just a moment please." Lisbet looked at Rayne. "Where did you go after you left Etta's and Harry's last night?"

Rebecca fidgeted in her seat, a reaction Rayne figured was clearly her saying she was uncomfortable being present at this exchange.

Rayne was shocked at the question, and a tad uncomfortable at the fact that it was asked in front of someone else, but without a moment's hesitation, she answered, "I drove the wagon back to the livery station and walked back to my room."

"You didn't stop at the saloon and see Maddie?" Lisbet asked flatly.

"No. Straight to my room. Why?"

Rebecca answered before Lisbet could, "I found Lisbet leanin' against a wall, cryin' her heart out. Seems Maddie approached her and told her that you spent the night with her. You can imagine the confusion and hurt Lisbet here felt after what she told me had been a wonderful afternoon with you."

"I see." Rayne took her hat off. "Lisbet, can we talk privately?" Rayne hoped Lisbet would agree, but understood if she might not want to.

"No, I think I'd like my friend Rebecca to stay," Lisbet replied, nervously.

"Alright, may I sit down?" And when Lisbet nodded, Rayne pulled out a chair and sat.

"I understand why you asked; I gave ya all the reason in the world. After I woke up from bein' shot and bangin' my head on that rock, I couldn't remember nothin' before bein' here in Telluride. I remembered Etta, and the folks here. I remembered bein' the deputy but nothin' else. One day, I asked why Maddie was bein' so nice and nursin' me and all. She told me it was cuz she loved me, that she and I were courtin', and that that's what ya do for the woman ya love. She said that no one here supported us, and that most would do anything to see that we weren't together. She said that Etta, especially, didn't want us happy, that she hated Maddie and that Harry would do or say anything that backed Etta. I believed her. Lisbet, please don't cry..." Rayne watched the tears start to fall from Lisbet's eyes.

"Keep going. I'm alright." Lisbet attempted to compose herself.

"Look, I know I can't make up for my mistake, and no amount of defendin' myself is gonna fix it. But I swear, I wasn't in my right mind when I slept with that woman. I never once felt about her the way I do about you, and even when I wasn't thinkin' straight, I knew my heart wasn't in it. I...it was physical, nothin' more." Rayne knew she wasn't making things any better. Hell, she even had to admit it sounded like a stretch.

She must have looked completely dejected, because Rebecca intervened with a hand on Rayne's arm. "Lisbet, I know that you got no reason to believe me, but I know Maddie real well. When she sets her mind on somethin', there's nothing much that's gonna stop her. Remember I told you that ya get to the point that ya can tell when someone's heart belongs elsewhere? Rayne always had that look to her. Even after Maddie wormed her way into Rayne's bed. When I see this woman look at you, I can see the love in her eyes. I never saw that when she looked at Maddie. In fact, come to think of it, I'd say the look she has where Maddie is

149

concerned reminds me of someone tryin' to get out of the way of a stampeding herd of wild pigs. Hm, maybe a den of snakes is a more accurate description. What do you think, Rayne? Do you think of Maddie as a wild pig or a bunch of snakes? I'm thinkin' snakes...she is a snake for sure. Hell, even pigs wouldn't want anything to do with her."

Lisbet choked on the tea she'd just sipped. Rayne just looked at Rebecca in shock.

"Oh come on, Rayne, admit it, you agree with me," Rebecca teasingly scolded.

Rayne shrugged her shoulders and tilted her head slightly. She wasn't about to disagree with Rebecca. The more Rayne thought about Maddie's actions, the more she saw that Maddie was indeed a snake in the grass. "You just might be right about that, Rebecca. Lisbet, fact is, yesterday was one of the best days I've had here. It was because I was with you and Ben. I ate supper with my family and dearest friends. I enjoyed laughin' and talkin', and when I left their place I went straight to my room and right to bed. Soon as my head hit the pillow I was out. This morning, I got up and went to the land office and was just gonna head out to look at some of the places up for sale. Why don't you come with me? You should have a say in how it looks and all. What do ya say, just you, me, and Ben? I'll have ya back before anyone knows you're gone. Come on, please? Think about it, finding *our* place, something that we can make our own."

"I suppose we could talk about what to do with your tart. I'm getting a little tired of her tellin' me how much fun you have with her and that I should leave you alone. It's just about time that she gets a taste of her own medicine."

"Does that mean you'll go with me? Check out some of the ranches with me?"

"Yes, I would like to see what you are envisioning for our ranch. I do need to go and see if Etta would mind watching Ben. I don't think he should be around for adult conversation. Rebecca, thank you so much for everything you've said and done. I do believe I'm hearin' what you're saying."

"Good, that snake can slither on to her next victim, unfortunately. Remember, ya just gotta decide who has the most to lose; them's the ones that likely don't play fair. Right about now, I'm thinkin' Maddie knows she is on the losin' end of things. Meanin' she is gonna say and do just about anything to make ya not believe in Rayne here. Now, ya'll head on out and have fun. I'll settle up with Martha." She reached for her glass of tea.

Rayne stood and stepped behind Lisbet's chair, her chivalrous side showing. She followed behind Lisbet as they exited the dining room and went to the mercantile to speak to Etta.

†

As they rode through the countryside, they made small talk. Occasionally, Rayne would ask a question about someone she happened to think about, like Tom or Bessie, and Lisbet would fill her in on what was going on with them before she had left Willow Spring.

Rayne kept her eyes focused on the road ahead of them. "Lisbet, just spit it out. I can see by the twitch in your jaw that ya got somethin' on your mind."

"I just been wonderin', since we left the dining room, but I ain't sure I wanna ask. Rayne...how? Were things with Maddie better than they were with me?"

151

"What? I don't..." Rayne stammered.

"I want to know, Rayne. I wanna understand why, if it wasn't something you enjoyed, it happened more than once. I can handle it. I promise I won't break down into a sobbin' mess. Least not in front of you."

"I ain't got a good answer for ya, Lisbet. I cain't tell ya that it was loneliness, cuz you dealt with it. I suppose the only answer I got is that I was weak. I let my body overrule my head and heart. Was it better than with you? No, fact is, she didn't satisfy me. It always left me with a hollow feelin'," Rayne replied, sorrow and regret in her voice.

"Then again, I ask, why did you keep doin' it?"

With a strained chuckle, Rayne replied, "Kept hopin' it'd end differently? I don't know, Lisbet. I do know that whatever the reason, it stopped when I stopped takin' the laudanum all the time. And I can promise you that it ain't gonna come back." Rayne looked at Lisbet.

Lisbet sighed, as she looked at Rayne and struggled with her fears and her desire to believe Rayne. She wanted to believe her, but she could still remember the pain she felt the moment she saw the redhead in Rayne's bed.

"Ya ain't gotta decide right now. I know it's gonna take some time. I just need to know that you'll give me a chance."

Lisbet looked away from the dark-haired woman. "I'm here with ya, ain't I?" She drew her gaze back.

"Yes, yes you are. One day at a time." Rayne smiled. A smile that was a mixture of sadness, longing, and relief. "Unless I miss my guess, that right there is the first ranch on my list." She pulled her horse to a stop and pointed ahead of them.

Before them, in a clearing, sat an expanse of lush, green grass, acres surrounded by a wooden split rail fence. There was a big ranch house, a large barn, and corrals nearby. On one side in the distance, you could see majestic, snowcapped mountain peaks, on the other tall aspens that in the fall would turn shades of yellows, oranges, and reds. The air held the aroma of sun-warmed, sweet wild flowers, and the silence was broken by the occasional chirp or chatter of insects. It was, in Rayne's mind, ideal. "Yup, this is almost perfect. What do you think, honey?"

"I think it has possibilities." Lisbet smiled. "Maybe we should ride on down and actually take a better look? Maybe, oh I don't know, walk around, take a good look at the house and barn. I mean, I think it would be good to know it's not gonna fall down on us, don't ya think?"

"Oh yeah, I guess that would be a good idea," Rayne said sheepishly. She had been so excited just seeing it. "Land office says there's a small fishin' pond on the property, as well as a hot spring. Last fall, when I arrived here, I met an injun who told me that the hot springs can help with all sort of ailments. That might be worth a try."

They rode down to the ranch. Just as Rayne suspected, it was amazingly beautiful. Rayne stopped at the barn and jumped off the wagon with the reins in her hand. She tethered the team to the fence.

Rayne reached up and placed her hands around Lisbet's waist and helped her down. With her hands still holding on to Lisbet, who stood in front of her, Rayne was lost. She was so close she could smell the soap Lisbet had used to wash up that morning. She could see the strong, steady beat of Lisbet's heart. And she could feel her own fingers trembling with the need to keep touching Lisbet.

It was Lisbet pulling away that brought Rayne back to her senses.

As her hands dropped, they each took a step back. Rayne tipped her head back and closed her eyes. There was no denying the attraction and desire that existed between them. Of course, that wasn't the issue. The issue was trust.

Rayne looked back at Lisbet. She couldn't blame the blonde; she accepted the way things had to be and acknowledged that it was going to take time to rebuild the trust she had broken. She reached for Lisbet's hand. "Let's go look at the house. Howard assured me it would be fine for us to walk through it."

With a sad smile, Lisbet reached for the outstretched hand and simply said, "Thank you."

Rayne gently gave the hand a squeeze. "I understand." She cleared her throat and continued, "So Howard, over at the land office, told me that the kitchen in this house is good sized, has one of them newer stoves, and has a water pump right in the kitchen. He says it's a damned nice home."

"Rayne watch your language," Lisbet teased.

Rayne mumbled, "Uh yeah, sorry about that." Lisbet simply chuckled.

As they walked through the main door, Lisbet's breath caught. The front door opened directly into a huge living area. The fireplace had been positioned in the center of one wall, with a beautiful pine mantel above it. Off to the right of the living area, was a doorway to what Lisbet found to be the kitchen. A stove sat against one wall, with cupboards and counters on one side. On the opposite wall stood an ice box, a sink, and a water pump. "Oh Lord,

Rayne, can you imagine not having to bring in buckets and buckets of water each day?"

"Yup, that would be somethin' wouldn't it? Let's take a look at the upstairs," Rayne suggested.

As they walked back into the living area, off the back wall were steps that led to the second floor. The upstairs was comprised of the bedrooms. A larger room overlooked the road and, off to the right, the entrance to the barn and corrals. Across the small hallway were three smaller rooms.

"This is huge, Rayne. What in the world would we ever do with all these rooms?" Lisbet asked.

"Ben needs his own room, and we'd have room for guests. I mean, I'd like Tom and Sally to visit us, maybe at some point my ma would come out...I don't know..." Rayne replied, as she thought about all the room in the house. She would love for her mother to visit. They had begun to communicate through letters after the death of her father but had yet to see each other. Whenever it did happen, Rayne wanted a room for her mother to stay, and this, to her way of thinking, was perfect.

"Oh I don't know, it's just so big," Lisbet said, as she walked around the room.

"Well we don't gotta decide right now, and there's still a couple of other places to look at, though none with the acreage this place has. But honestly, just considerin' the price they want for this ranch, this is the better deal. I swear, some folks are just out to rob a person blind." Rayne walked to the window. "Come look at this, darlin'."

Lisbet walked over to where Rayne was and looked out the window.

"Over by the barn." Rayne watched Lisbet's reaction to the sight in front of them, she smiled.

In the meadow near the barn stood a doe with her two fawns, who were busy playing. The doe would lower her head, take a mouthful of grass, then look up with a watchful eye on her babies as she chewed.

For Rayne, nothing in her wildest imagination could be better than seeing Lisbet watch the scene below them. Rayne reached out and wiped the tear that fell from Lisbet's green eye. "What is it, darlin'?" Rayne stepped behind and wrapped her arms around the blonde.

"It's just…it's beautiful and perfect, and I'm tryin' to figure out how to forgive you. God, I want to, Rayne. I'm just so afraid. I can't…I can't have my heart broken like that again," Lisbet cried, her chest heaving through the tears as she lost the battle to contain them.

"I know, darlin'. I won't ever put you in the position to have it broken ever again," Rayne said into Lisbet's hair.

Lisbet turned in Rayne's arms and buried her face. Her tears fell into the blue fabric of Rayne's shirt. Through her sobs, she asked, "Do you have any idea what it did to me to see that woman in your bed?"

Rayne's shame burned in her heart. How was she supposed to answer that without it sounding like she was just begging for forgiveness? So she answered the only way she could, "Darlin', I know how I woulda felt. And I know how hard it woulda been for me to understand and forgive. And the fact that I put you in a place that ya gotta decide that is unforgivable to me. I cain't begin to tell ya how ashamed I am that I slept with her and that I hurt you like I have."

"Damn you, Rayne, why can't I just walk away from you? Why does it hurt to breathe when I even think about it?" Lisbet pounded her fist into Rayne's shoulder.

"Maybe for the same reason I cain't imagine a life without you, cuz you are my life."

The couple stood there for a while with Lisbet letting her tears fall and Rayne just holding her. Rayne knew one thing and one thing only, should Lisbet forgive her, she would never put her through this kind of pain ever again.

Eventually, the tears ended. While Rayne offered to head back to town, Lisbet insisted that they stay and walk around the rest of the ranch. Through the huge barn and corrals to the pasture, Lisbet had to agree it was indeed beautiful. She watched Rayne and knew without a doubt that Rayne wanted this place. While it was going to take some time, Lisbet knew in her heart that her family would live and be happy here. She could see them laughing in the living area in front of the fireplace. She would be mending socks while Rayne read to Ben. She could see herself and Rayne upstairs making love, as Ben slept across the hall. "Rayne why don't we get the horses and ride along the fence? I'd like to see the rest of the place." She smiled when she saw Rayne's face light up.

Lisbet was truly amazed at how large the ranch was. There were sectioned off areas to accommodate moving the cattle, as well as fields for growing corn or hay. Lisbet was impressed with the place, and though she knew they should at least look at other ranches, she knew this was the one. "Rayne, how about we take a look at the barn again? We should probably know what the loft looks like before we make a decision. I mean, I know we got other places to look at, but that should be somethin' we keep in mind."

Lisbet reached for Rayne's hand for help up the final rung of the ladder that led to the loft of the barn. Up against the wall that Lisbet faced were bales of hay that had been left when the previous owner moved out of the area, and the floor boards were covered with layers of loose hay.

Once Lisbet was on the floor, Rayne put her hands on her hips and looked around. She carefully walked to the far end of the barn, inspecting beams and joints, while Lisbet walked to the large doors that stood open to the expanse of land down below. "It looks to be sound." Lisbet leaned her shoulder against the door frame.

Rayne walked up behind her. "Will ya look at that view." She took in the unblocked view of the valley below them and the acres that surrounded the ranch.

Lisbet walked to a bale and sat down. She bit on her bottom lip. "We'll have to keep Ben from comin' up here."

Rayne looked her and smiled. "Yup, for a while anyways. Ya know the boy's gonna explore, whether we want him to or not. We just gotta make sure he understands not to come up here unless he is with me."

Rayne strolled to the bales and sat next to Lisbet. As she pulled a strand of hay from the bale, she leaned back and crossed her ankles. She stuck an end of the hay in her mouth and locked her hands behind her head. "Damn, it's so peaceful out here." She looked out at the meadow below. "Look over there, momma and her babies are still here."

Lisbet leaned against Rayne. "Maybe they like us bein' here."

"Maybe." Rayne put her arm around Lisbet's shoulder and pulled her in tighter. She closed her eyes as she inhaled the scent of Lisbet's hair. It hit her again just how much she missed the closeness they had shared. She knew she would never tire of being this close to Lisbet.

God help her, each time she got close to Lisbet she wanted her more. She wanted Lisbet in her arms, she wanted to feel Lisbet's lips on hers, she wanted, no, she needed to feel Lisbet's body next to hers.

Lisbet could feel the heat coming from Rayne's body. As much as she wanted to deny it, she felt safe with Rayne. She missed the feel of the strong arms around her, the way Rayne's body felt against hers. She missed the way Rayne touched her. Lisbet shifted on the bale, leaned towards Rayne, closed the space between them, and kissed her.

The kiss was gentle, almost shy. Lisbet's heart was beating rapidly as she trembled. She wanted to keep kissing the woman she loved. She wanted the images of Maddie lying in Rayne's bed out of her mind. She wanted to put this all behind her. She was afraid though, but at the moment that didn't keep her from placing another kiss on Rayne's lips.

It was only when Rayne kissed her back that she let herself begin to let go of the anxiety she felt and went in the direction her body wanted to go. She deepened her kiss, even as her hands shakily caressed Rayne's face.

Before Rayne could realize what was happening, Lisbet undid her jeans, unbuttoned her shirt, and pressed them back into the hay.

It was late afternoon when they headed back to Harry and Etta's, completely ignoring the events in the barn.

†

Rayne rode into town around sundown, her mood the best it had been in a very long time. That mood held, right up until Maddie ran up and wrapped her arms around Rayne's neck.

"Where you been all day, darlin'? I've been missin' ya." She attempted to pull Rayne into a kiss.

Rayne pulled back. Her hands reached for the arms that were around her neck and pulled them down. "What part of stay away from me do you not understand?" she asked through clenched teeth.

"You don't mean that; I know you're just sayin' that to keep that woman happy. Although I don't get why you just don't tell her that you don't want her no more." Maddie placed a hand on a hip. She placed her other hand on Rayne's taut stomach and slowly moved it up, as her eyes suggestively looked Rayne up and down.

Rayne's hand shot up and stopped the hand. "Maddie ya gotta stop. I'm sorry, but I know exactly what I want. And it ain't you. I need ya to understand, it's you I don't want no more. Now stay away from me, don't approach me, and don't talk to me. It's the last time I'm tellin' ya."

Right as she finished, Hawks walked up to them. "Evenin' Miz Maddie, how ya doin'?"

"I'm doin' alright, Sheriff, just tryin' to convince your deputy to come have a drink or two with me, and she won't agree. Tell her it's just a couple drinks, would ya?" Maddie pouted at Hawks.

"Miz Maddie, I'd love to be able to tell Deputy Mathews here to go have a drink with ya, but I actually got some business I need to discuss with her. So do ya mind terribly if I steal her away?"

The expression on her face fell slightly. "Oh, I suppose not, after all, it is business. I'll be waitin' for ya if ya wanna head over after you're done."

"Don't count on it." Rayne moved past Maddie with indifference.

†

Rayne waited until she and Hawks were a good distance from the redhead. "Thanks, I wasn't sure how I was gonna get away from her without gettin' nasty."

"Yeah, Maddie can be somewhat overwhelming. I gotta ask ya, what are you gonna do?"

"Hell, Clinton, I ain't got no idea what to do about her. *You* got any idea?" Rayne walked along with the sheriff, her hands in her pockets.

"Sorry, I ain't got none. I take it by that little encounter back there that she ain't agreein' with you breakin' up with her?"

"She is under the impression that I'm head over heels with her, and that I just ain't figured out how to break it to Lisbet. Clinton, how the hell did I get myself into this damned mess?"

"Yeah, I've been wonderin' that myself. How did the land lookin' go?" Hawks opened the door to the sheriff's office. Once inside, he walked to his desk, opened the bottom drawer, and pulled out a bottle of bourbon. He placed it on his desk and walked to the stove, where he grabbed the two tin coffee cups.

"I rode out to the old Hamilton ranch. I gotta tell ya, I fell in love with the place. It's exactly what I dreamt of. Hell, I think Lisbet likes it as well. Though she didn't right out say so. Honestly, I ain't sure where we even stand."

"Ya sure do know how to make a mess of things, don't ya Mathews? Was ya always like this or is it something new since comin' to this here fair town?"

"Honestly Hawks, I don't think I can answer. I feel like I been messin' up things my whole life." Rayne reached for the bottle and poured some into each cup.

"Na, I don't believe that, Mathews." Hawks thought about some of the things Rayne had confided to him, like the reasons that led her to her uncle's ranch in Willow Springs, about her and the shooting that killed her father. There was no doubt in his mind that Rayne had been dealt a lousy hand in her young life. He'd also gotten to know the woman and knew her to be a hardworking, honest woman. "I believe that the Lord intends to make sure you come through all your troubles. He's seen the kinda person ya are, that's what matters. Now, I ain't sayin' that it's gonna be easy. Hell, ya already know that all the bad stuff just ensures that you appreciate the good, and ya do, that's for damned sure."

"I wish for once the Lord would let me have it a tad easier." Rayne took a drink of the liquor. She closed her eyes and held her head back, and let the liquid warm her. "Just once, ya know?"

"What doesn't kill us makes us stronger…" Hawks replied.

"That's what they say. Hey, thanks for rescuin' me." Rayne placed the cup on the desk and pushed out of her chair. "I'm gonna head to my room and try to get some sleep. I'll see ya in the mornin'."

"Yup. Oh, glad ya had a good day with your wife. She seems like a good woman; I'd hate to see ya lose her."

Rayne smiled, as she placed her hand on the doorknob. "That she is. And I'm doin' my damnedest to keep that from happenin'."

"Think I'll head over to the saloon, have a word with Rebecca," Hawk spoke the words to no one in particular, as he too stood up and headed for the door. Once outside, Rayne headed one way and Hawks the other.

†

Hawks walked through the swinging doors and glanced around before he headed towards the bar, his spurs clanking on the wooden floor. "Howdy Jonas, set me up with a bottle of whiskey why don't ya." He tossed a couple of coins on the bar.

As he was pouring some in a glass, Maddie approached him from behind. "Well, Sheriff, I hope you're happy with yourself."

Hawks took a breath, as he set the bottle down and picked up his glass. He brought the glass to his lips. "Yeah, I reckon I sure as hell am. Why do set your sights on my deputy?"

"Why not? She intrigues me, and honestly, because I want her."

Hawks cleared his throat and turned to face the woman. "I see. So, I suppose the fact that she's told ya more than once that she ain't got no interest in you and she don't want you no more, means nothin' to ya?"

163

"She ain't got no idea what she wants!"

"That's where you'd be wrong. Now, Rayne is a hell of a deputy, and one fine, upstandin' human being. She's been through a lot and deserves a little happiness. So I'm only gonna say this to ya once, and I suggest you listen and listen well. Ya leave Rayne alone, ya stop behavin' as though ya got a claim on her, and ya stop tryin' to make her life miserable. She is gonna try to make things work with her wife, and you're gonna stay away from 'em. Is that clear?"

Maddie tossed her head and laughed. "Well now, Sheriff, that almost sounds as if you're tryin' to tell me what to do. That ain't what you're tryin' to do is it, Sheriff?"

With a smile that didn't reach his eyes, he replied, "Yeah, yeah that might be what I'm tryin' to do. I mean if ya wanna take it that way, the other way ya can take it is that I'm givin' ya a warnin'."

"I'll take it into consideration, Sheriff." Maddie turned and walked away.

"Clinton, are you tryin' to give Maddie a hard time?" Rebecca approached the sheriff.

Clinton watched, as the redhead walked towards a table full of gamblers. "I'm tryin' to keep my deputy married. I tell ya, that there woman is trouble."

"She's a snake. I feel bad for Rayne gettin' mixed up with her. Ya really don't believe she is gonna walk away from Rayne, do ya?" Rebecca ran her hand over his strong shoulder.

"No, I don't. Honestly, I believe Rayne would have to die to get away from that bitch."

"Come on, let's go upstairs." Rebecca reached for the bottle and his hand.

Chapter Fourteen

Rayne and Lisbet didn't see each other much for the next week or so. With Rayne's duties as deputy taking up her days, it was difficult for her to ride out to Etta and Harry's place. Of course, that also meant that she didn't see Ben either. So after dealing with Ben asking repeatedly to see his ma, Lisbet decided to take a ride into town with him.

Maddie was standing at the saloon door that afternoon, joking and flirting with the men who walked by. She spotted Lisbet and the little boy walking towards the sheriff's office. She pushed away from the doorway and began to walk towards the blonde woman, shouting, "Why don't you just go back where you came from? Ain't you got it yet, Rayne don't want you no more."

Lisbet kept her gaze straight ahead, ignoring the taunts of the redhead and telling Ben to pay no mind and to keep walkin'.

Maddie grabbed a hold of her hair. With a screech of pain, Lisbet reached for the hand, as she tried to spin around. Her hand struck out and connected with Maddie's cheek. Maddie squealed in shock and immediate anger that Lisbet would strike her and, in true Maddie fashion, slapped back. The fight was on.

Before long, a group had gathered, bets were made, and shouts began to fill the air. Men were shouting at each of them to look out and laughing along with an occasional ouch. The commotion drifted into the sheriff's office.

As Rayne reached the street, she looked to her left, saw the crowd, the fight, and ran over to stop it. As she reached the gathering and made her way to the fight, she was surprised to see that it was two women, and stunned when she realized that one of the women was Lisbet. She was so surprised that it took her a second or two to react. Once she did, her shouts to stop went unheard. Rayne ended up having to step between the two and was rewarded with a hand hitting her square on her jaw. That's when she spun around and wrapped an arm around one woman's waist and lifted her up while taking a couple of steps forward. Luckily for Rayne, it was Lisbet she picked up. Someone from the crowd had managed to grab Maddie and pull her away as well.

Rayne managed to stop the hand that quickly approached her face. "Stop this nonsense right now."

Lisbet's eyes blazed dark with anger and her chest heaved up and down with each breath she took.

"Just what in the hell is goin' on here?" Rayne asked through the surge of anger caused by her rush of adrenalin. Her angry gaze moved from Lisbet to Maddie, then back to Lisbet.

Maddie jerked out of the hands that held her back and moved closer to Rayne shouting, "It was her! She saw me standin' there and started shoutin' obscenities at me and then attacked me. I had to fight back to protect myself." Maddie wiped at an imaginary tear.

At Maddie's words, Lisbet lunged at the redhead and screamed, "You lyin' bitch."

Rayne was quick and was able to grab Lisbet again around her waist. "I said stop!" she ordered and turned towards Maddie with a finger pointed. "Enough." She turned to Lisbet and asked in a quieter, softer tone. "Are ya alright?" Lisbet nodded, and Rayne continued, "What happened? And I'm askin' her," she said before Maddie could interrupt.

"Ben and I...Oh my God, where's Ben? Ben!" Lisbet shouted, as she spun around searching the crowd.

It was Rebecca who called back, "I got him, and he's safe."

Lisbet was visibly relieved, and she continued, "We was on our way to see you, when we passed the saloon that...woman, began yellin' rude things at me. I told Ben to pay her no mind and keep walkin', then all of a sudden she grabbed a hold of my hair and started hittin' me."

Rayne took a deep breath. With one hand on her hip, she pushed back her hat, as she looked around at the remaining crowd. "Ya'll head on about your business, this here is over." She looked back at Maddie and caught a smugness that just irritated her beyond belief.

When Rayne turned to look at her, Lisbet could see the anger in the ice-blue eyes. "Ya'll head back to Etta's," Rayne said. "Iffin' ya need to do some shoppin', tell me. I'll come get ya and we'll go."

Lisbet softly replied, "No, we were comin' to see you, nothin' else. Ben…we've missed you was all."

"Really? You've missed me? Not just Ben?" Rayne seemed almost afraid to hear the answer.

"Yes, I've missed you." Lisbet blushed a tad.

"Okay, ya'll head back to Etta's. I'll come by this evenin' if that's all right with ya."

Lisbet smiled. "Supper will be waitin' for ya." She turned to find Rebecca and Ben.

Before Lisbet had even walked five steps, Rayne was grabbing Maddie's arm roughly and pulling her towards the sheriff's office.

"Ouch, Rayne, you're hurtin' my arm. Rayne, slow down."

"Shut up," Rayne said coldly, as her grip tightened just a bit more.

"Rayne, please, you're hurtin' me."

"Ask me if I give a damn," Rayne was beyond furious when they reached the sheriff's office. She pulled open the door and pushed Maddie inside, towards a jail cell. "Get in there."

Maddie stopped abruptly and turned to look disbelievingly at Rayne. "What? You want me to get in there?" She pointed to the cell.

Rayne looked at Maddie. "It's where I put the drunk and disorderly."

"But I'm not…"

Rayne stopped her before she continued. "Stop talkin'. No, you aren't drunk, but you were disorderly. If ya wanna go around fightin' in the streets, then ya might wanna get used to the scenery from in here. Now, step inside." Rayne held open the cell door.

"Wait a damned minute, I wasn't the only one fightin'," Maddie replied angrily.

"No, ya weren't, but from what I'm hearin' from folks in the street, you sure as heck started it," Sheriff Hawks said gruffly as he walked in.

"Ya wanna place her under arrest for disturbing the peace, Deputy?"

Maddie began to weep and walked towards the sheriff. "Sheriff, please, I don't know what came over me. I ain't never done nothin' like this before, and if ya can see your way past all this mess, I promise I won't never do it again." She approached the man, her hand softly touching his worn, tan shirt.

Rayne watched the woman work and rolled her eyes. She couldn't believe she'd let herself believe anything the woman had ever said to her. More to the point, she was disgusted with herself that she'd allowed herself to be tricked by her.

"What do ya think, Rayne?" Hawks reached up and grabbed the hand that was roaming over his chest and pushed it away from him. His eyes were on Rayne,and a smile twitched at the corner of his mouth.

Maddie turned to look at Rayne and pouted. "Honest, Rayne, I apologize for my behavior. Please, don't put me in that cell."

Rayne shook her head as she smirked. "Maddie, if ya think for one second that I'm gonna believe anything ya say to me anymore, ya got another think comin'." With a deep sigh, she closed the cell door. "Fine. I ain't gonna put ya in jail this time. But I swear to God almighty, the next time I won't hesitate. Do ya understand me?"

"I surely do, Rayne, thank you," Maddie responded with a smile, as she took a step for the door.

"Maddie, I know I done warned ya about stayin' away from Lisbet and my boy. Up to now, I've let it all go. But I'm here to tell ya in front of the sheriff, stay away from them." Rayne's voice was ice.

With a smug smile, Maddie stopped at the door. "Why, Rayne, I didn't approach them. I swear, this time, she approached me. I don't care what she told ya...at least that's my story."

Rayne took off her hat, threw it on her desk, and walked briskly to the window.

Hawks walked to his desk, his heels striking the wooden floorboards with his steps. His chair squeaked as he sat down. "So what're ya gonna do about that one there?" He put his feet on his desk and leaned back and laced his fingers behind his head.

"Hell if I know. But God dammit, I feel like I need to chew off my arm or somethin' to get free from her." Rayne walked to her desk and sat down. She looked at Clinton. He was a good man, and she couldn't imagine him being in a situation like this. "Hawks, what would you do if you were in my position?"

With a chuckle, he replied, "Oh, I wouldn't have been stupid enough to be caught in the position you're in."

"Thanks a lot. Really, how in the hell do I get myself out of this mess? Ya know I really didn't know what the hell I was doin' when I took to her bed. Ya know when I came here it was to make a better life for my family, to expand my ranch. I took this job, cuz I needed the work, and I figured that folks would maybe open up to me. And they did, ya know, I actually started makin' friends, more than just Harry and Etta. Then one day I go and get shot. I wake up to realize that I cain't remember shit, and I'm sleepin' with that redheaded devil. Next thing I know, all hell's breakin' loose when Lisbet opened my door. I remembered her and things start to fall into place and make sense."

"Like what things." Hawks swung his feet off the desk and leaned forward.

"I'd have these images of this blonde and a ranch and dreams. God, I'd have these dreams and in them I was so damned happy. I could remember us laughin' and livin' this perfect life, ya know? I felt this peace that I cain't even begin to describe.

"I took one look at her standin' outside that door and knew everything I ever wanted in life was about to walk outta my life, because I'd messed up and allowed that snake to slither into my bed. Now, every time Lisbet comes into town, Maddie is hurling insults at her or insinuating things that ain't true."

"Always did think that Maddie would bring a shit load a trouble for anyone who decided to get involved with her. Always seemed to be a tad high strung, too possessive for my tastes. Hell, I reckon that goes for all the guys around these parts." Hawks laughed as he said the last part. "Sorry to say, Rayne, I'm thinkin' the only way you're gonna be free of that one, is for her to either mosey on from here or you do. And I'd hate for you to be the one."

Rayne pushed away from her desk. "Not goin' anywhere, except for supper this evenin' with Lisbet and my son. I'm gonna make my rounds and make sure I'm caught up on my work here and head out for what I'm hopin' will be a fine evenin'."

"Alright, just keep clear of that redhead, ya hear?"

171

"That's my plan boss."

†

Maddie waltzed into the saloon. She put a sway to her hips and a bigger smile on her face for the few men who whistled and cheered at her, but she was fuming inside. How dare Rayne take that woman's word over hers? And then to yank her around by her arm into the sheriff's office and threaten to toss her into a jail cell. Maddie was livid at that treatment. *Oh you'll pay for that blondie, just you wait and see.* She continued to smile and flirt with the men.

Rebecca watched as Maddie made her way around the room. She made certain she was available to speak to the woman when she approached the bar for drinks.

"That was quite the display out there," Rebecca said in a friendly and calm voice.

"Wasn't it? I just can't tell ya how shocked I was at that woman's behavior." Maddie placed her hand over her heart and a look of shock slipped onto her face.

Rebecca reached out and placed a hand on Maddie's arm as she leaned closer. "What happened? I mean, I'm sitting in here then all of a sudden people are shoutin' about a fight outside. Can ya imagine my surprise when I see that you're involved?"

Maddie was eager to tell her spin on the events that led to her street brawl. "Oh my, I'm just so shaken! I was standin' there talkin' to folks outside, when she saw me and just started to shout such horrible things at me. And with her son in tow! I just can't..." Maddie added a shake to her voice and hand.

Had Rebecca not known the woman as well as she did, she would have fallen for the act. Playing along, Rebecca placed a hand to her heart and gasped, "Oh my, how horrible. Am I correct that the deputy stepped between the two of you?"

"Yes, she did and…" Maddie looked around her as if she was about to say something secret. "Rayne is such a sweet woman, I know she wouldn't want everyone to know how worried about me she was, but she escorted me to the sheriff's office just to make sure I was alright. And to make sure that evil woman had left town before I came back here. I tell ya, I am truly afraid for my life."

"Oh my, I can't imagine." Rebecca saw Hawks walk into the saloon. "Well, honey, I know you're safe now, and I see some thirsty men waitin' for them drinks and your attention. Young Billy over there is lookin' like a love-sick puppy. You best go put the boy outta his misery," she said with a smile.

"That poor boy, I suppose he deserves some attention." Maddie turned to look at the young man, who indeed looked at her like a lost puppy. With a chuckle, she winked at him then touched Rebecca's arm. "Thank you for caring about my safety."

"Of course, honey, us girls have to stick together." Rebecca thought for sure her sarcasm was clearly heard.

Hawks walked towards Rebecca, watching Maddie walk away. "So what's she sayin'?"

"Oh, you wouldn't believe me if I told ya."

"Knowin' her, yeah, I would." Hawks motioned for a glass from the busy barkeep.

"How's Rayne?" Rebecca asked, concern clearly in her voice.

"Regrettin' the day she met Maddie and surprisingly in a good mood, considerin' her wife was just in a catfight. Seems they're havin' supper this evenin', and she's really excited. Let's just hope that one will leave well enough alone for the moment."

"That's good to hear. I'm worried about Lisbet."

"Why, darlin'?" Hawks turned to face Rebecca, and leaned against the bar.

"Let's go somewhere more private." Rebecca reached for both glasses and moved away from the bar, heading to a far table in a corner. Clinton followed.

He pulled a chair out for her and sat beside her. "What's on your mind, darlin'?"

"I ain't known Lisbet long, but the few times I've spoken to her, there's one thing that is clear. She adores that little boy. For her to be involved in a fight like that in front of him worries me. Just hearin' her talk, ya know she adores Rayne too, and honestly, if I was in her position, I'd be ready to kill anyone that hurt my family like Maddie has."

Clinton frowned as a worrisome thought formed. "Ya don't believe she would really kill Maddie, do ya?"

"I'd lean more towards Rayne doin' that than Lisbet, but I don't see Lisbet takin' much more from Maddie. That woman is causin' some bad heartache."

"Ah, there ain't no use borrowin' trouble. Rayne is a mighty fine woman, she would rather cut her arm off than to hurt anyone, least not without some regret or pain. I got a lot a faith in my deputy to do the right thing," Hawks said with complete conviction. He did have total trust in his deputy to do what was right. He hoped he could trust her to do the right thing where Maddie was concerned as well.

†

Rayne walked to her hotel and went to her room to wash up. As she poured water in the wash basin she whistled a tune. She had a good feeling about tonight, and the thought of Lisbet missin' her made her smile even bigger. She splashed water on her face, then found her dress shirt and a clean pair of jeans. Before long, she had her boots on and was heading towards the livery and her horse, totally unaware of the eyes that watched as she rode out of town.

†

Supper that evening comprised of a tasty pork roast, mashed potatoes, a delicious gravy made from the drippings of the roast, some glazed carrots, and lemonade. Desert was a warm apple pie and coffee. And while Rayne enjoyed the company of her friends, she was most happy that she was with Ben and Lisbet. Ben spent the evening bouncing up and down in his seat, giggling, and was generally disruptive, in a happy kid way.

After several times of telling Ben to settle down, Rayne decided to take things into her own hands. "What do you say you, me, and Momma go for a walk?"

"Yea, wet's go, wet's go!! Mon Momma, mon…" Ben jumped up and down with excitement.

"What do you say, Lis, wanna go for a walk?" Rayne asked hopefully.

Lisbet smiled as she looked at Rayne and Ben, who were both watching her. "Sure, why not. I definitely do need to walk this meal off. I feel like I've gained a hundred pounds."

"Well come on, let's get goin'." Rayne responded with a big smile. Together, the three of them bid goodbye to Harry and Etta and headed out the door.

Somewhere along the walk, Rayne and Lisbet began holding hands, as they watched Ben run ahead of them. The topic of the fight was ignored. They just walked.

Lisbet pulled Rayne to a stop. "Rayne, have ya been able to go look at anymore ranches?"

"No...I been busy, so I ain't had a chance to. Why?"

Lisbet reached for Rayne's head, pulled it down, and gently placed a kiss on her lips. When she pulled away she whispered, "I think we need to find our own place. Unless ya don't want me no more, I mean, I know I ain't thin like I used to be but..."

Rayne immediately placed a finger on Lisbet's lips. "Woman, are you crazy? Ain't I been tryin' to convince ya that you're the one my heart belongs to? Ain't I been doin' whatever I can think of to prove to ya that I made a mistake with the whore?" Rayne's voice grew incredulous.

Lisbet cleared her throat, grabbed Rayne's shirt, and pulled her close, whispering against her lips, "I know you have been." She gave the dark-haired woman a deep kiss. "Now let's get our son, and a home. It's time we get our family back together. What do you say, Deputy Mathews?"

With a giant smile and a spring in her spirit, Rayne nodded enthusiastically. "I sure as hell think that's a fine idea. Um, so do you...wanna move to the hotel with me? I mean...I don't...I don't wanna...am I takin' too much for granted here?"

176

"I really wanna be with ya. I can't tell ya how much I wanna be with ya, but I can't do that. Not with that woman right there."

Rayne kicked at a rock on the ground, as she thought about what she had just asked the woman she loved to do. "I'm sorry, I shouldn't have asked that. I'll see what I can do about findin' us a place."

"We will find us a place." Lisbet reached up and touched Rayne's face tenderly.

"So, uh, not that I ain't grateful and all, but what made ya decide to give us another chance?"

"Rayne, I don't know if I can forget what ya done, and I can't promise that it ain't gonna pop up into my head from time to time. But try as I might, I can't imagine my life without you. I don't want to. I talked to Rebecca the other day, and she told me something that I ain't been able to forget. I started to remember my days back when I was growin' up at the saloon. The girls, well, they would talk about the guys who always just went in for a drink and to play cards. How there was this look to 'em that just said their hearts belonged to someone and ain't no one was gonna change that. Rebecca told me that she's seen that look in your eyes. I know I seen it too, I just chose to ignore it."

Rayne nodded as she listened to what Lisbet said. She took a step towards Lisbet, who had just turned to catch Ben as he ran to her. A gunshot rang out, and the bullet whizzed by, striking a tree. "Jesus Christ," Rayne exclaimed, as she hit her knee and reached for the holstered gun. "Stay down, and stay put." She rushed towards the direction the gunshot had come from.

"Rayne…" Lisbet shouted.

Rayne turned slightly, "I said to stay there." She turned back and headed into the darkness.

It was too dark to see or find anything, so she went back to Lisbet and Ben. "Are you two alright?" She ran to them and scooped them up in her arms. Only when Lisbet and Ben were in her arms did she stopped shaking.

"We're fine, Rayne. Just take us home. Please."

"Ben, son, are ya alright?" Rayne pushed him out to arm's length and tried to look him over. In the light from the quarter moon, Rayne could barely see the boy nod. "Good, okay, let's get back to Harry and Etta's place. I'm damned sure whoever was out there is gone, and I ain't gonna find anything in the dark." Rayne led the way back to Harry's house.

†

"I need to put Ben to bed. Will you wait to leave till I come back down?"

"Yeah, I'll wait." Rayne kneeled down and reached for her son. "I love ya son, and I'll see ya tomorrow okay?" When the boy nodded, she drew him into a hug. "Good, now you get some sleep and listen to your mama, ya hear?"

Lisbet smiled. "Come along, Ben. I'll be right back."

Rayne watched Lisbet walk up the steps with their son. When they'd reached the top, she turned to the study where Harry was sitting with the paper and glass of whiskey. "Uh, Harry, can I talk to ya for a minute?" She took a step towards the entry way.

Harry put the paper down. "Of course, Rayne, come on in. What's on your mind?" He stood up and went to the credenza where he reached for a glass and the bottle of whiskey.

"I need ya to keep Lisbet and Ben safe. Someone just took a shot at us out there." Rayne accepted the drink.

"Oh shit, any idea who?"

"No, it was too dark for me to see anything and way too dark to track whoever it was. Right now, I ain't sure who they were aiming at. I can only assume it was me. In which case, it's safer if I stay away."

"What do you mean, it's safer if you stay away?" Lisbet interrupted, as she walked into the room.

"I ah…I don't know who shot at us, and I can't take the risk of whoever it was tryin' again and hittin' you or Ben." Rayne looked to Harry for help.

"No, this isn't…we need to talk about this." Lisbet put her hands on her hips.

"I need to keep you and our son safe, and I ain't doin' that if I'm bein' shot at. I gotta figure out who took a shot at us just now. Until I do, it ain't safe," Rayne said in defense of her decision.

"I don't believe this…didn't we just talk about puttin' our family back together under one roof? And now here ya are makin' decisions again that impact us without discussion." Lisbet's voice rose in anger.

"Harry what…"

"No. Do not bring Harry into this." Lisbet's eyes blazed with anger.

"I just uh…" Harry cleared his throat then continued, "So, I'm only gonna say this, then I'll leave you two alone to discuss this. But I see Rayne's point. It's one thing to know you're in danger, but for someone ya love to be in danger because of you is something totally different."

"Is that so?" Lisbet shot back at the man. "Is that why you let Etta traipse all over God's creation alone? Lord knows you weren't with her when she found shelter in our barn, were you?"

Harry ran a hand through his hair as he turned red. "No...No, you're right Lisbet, and I'm here to tell ya that had anything bad happened to her, I'd never be able to forgive myself. So, I understand where Rayne is comin' from. I'll leave you two now. Um let me just get my paper and whiskey." Harry sidestepped away from Lisbet, grabbed his paper and glass, and sidestepped her again as he headed out the door. "I'll make sure we keep an ear out for Ben," he said as an afterthought.

"Lisbet, I know..." Rayne began.

"No, you don't know. I didn't fight to keep you in Willow Springs; I allowed you to talk me into lettin' you come to this godforsaken place. A place where you allowed someone else in your bed. I'm willin' to forgive you that. However I will not, *will not* forgive you not discussin' this with me. We make this decision together, or Ben and I get back on that train and go home."

"Dammit, Lisbet, I cannot and will not put yours or Ben's life in danger." Rayne held her hand on her hip above her gun belt.

"Rayne, when we met I was a on the street, stealin' to get through the night, sleepin' in alleys and barns, hopin' and prayin' that I didn't get shot by the owner thinkin' I was tryin' to steal his horse or something. I set out with our son, traveled alone on a train here, and you don't believe that was dangerous? You don't think every day in this world is dangerous?"

"I..."

"I'm not done. Do you recall your days on the trail ridin' to the ranch? Did that ever seem dangerous to you? Or did that not count?"

"Lisbet, you don't understand. I wouldn't be able to live with myself if anything ever happened to you or Ben because of me."

"I understand that. But I promised to be by your side no matter what, through the good and the bad. We make our life here together, from here on out. If not, then they win." Lisbet motioned to the outside world. "I swear to God, I will not allow Maddie to think she's beat us."

"Ok. But there has to be some rules. And one of the rules has to be that you and Ben don't go anywhere alone. You learn to shoot, and you wear a gun."

"Rayne, I can't let her or anyone change who I am."

"Dammit, Lisbet, I can't trust that I'll always be there in time. Dammit. Right now, all I can think of and remember is Dobson. Ya remember him? I barely made it back home in time to keep you safe."

Lisbet looked at Rayne and saw the pain and fear in her eyes. She remembered James Dobson, a deputy back in Willow Springs who had attempted to molest her one day when Rayne was out checking the herd. Dobson was a hateful man who held nothing but contempt for Rayne and was set on causing her pain. Rayne barely made it home in time. Lisbet remembered the day clearly.

Dobson had ridden up to the Rockin M Ranch looking for trouble. Lisbet thought the approaching rider was Rayne and ran out to greet her. She would always remember his arrival clearly. She didn't like him and didn't trust him. Afraid, she ran for the house.

"Where ya goin'? You ain't bein' very hospitable now, are ya? I think maybe someone needs to teach you some manners, teach you how to respect a man. Now see, I think that's your entire problem. Ya ain't got no one to teach you what a man expects. What do you get from that bitch anyways? Seems to me she is missin' the proper equipment."
He laughed at his own crude joke. "Oh hell, it don't matter. I'm about to teach you all you need to know." He sneered as he pushed her into the house, pushing her to the bedroom, his hand tight on her arm. He stood at the bedroom door, staring at her, as his hands worked the buckle of his gun belt. He let it drop to the floor, and the thud echoed in the house. Lisbet froze. Her mind screamed for her to run, but her body just couldn't obey. He approached her, his hands on the buttons of his pants, undoing them one by one. When he got within a foot of her, she screamed and swung her hand at him. The blow barely grazed his face, his however, connected with her cheek. She felt the back of his hand strike her right cheek, and she fell back onto the bed. He descended on her, his hand pushing the hem of the dress up and pulling at her undergarments. That's as far as he got, before he was pulled off and thrown across the room.

Lisbet sighed. "Yes my love, I remember that man. But most of all, I remember you. I remember you, so strong, so brave, so lovin' and carin'. I remember your arms wrappin' around me and me feelin' so safe. I've never stopped feelin' that way, Rayne. I will not, I refuse to feel any differently now."

Rayne hung her head, knowing that there would be no talking Lisbet into wearing a gun, and there would be no convincing her to keep their distance. With a resigned sigh she said, "Ok."

"I think I know, cuz I love you just as much. I just hope you're right about this." Rayne kissed the top of Lisbet's head. "I should go. I need to tell Hawks about our bein' shot at. Need to figure out who tried to shoot us."

"Rayne, I don't wanna be alone tonight."

"I don't either, but I can't—I wouldn't feel right stayin' here, and ya can't leave Ben tonight." Rayne hated saying no.

"You're right, I'm just bein' selfish." Lisbet was a little ashamed that she had even suggested that.

"Darlin', I'm gonna head back to town and go see just what Maddie was up to this evenin'. She's the one I'd lay money would try to shoot me."

Lisbet touched Rayne's face again before giving her a kiss to her cheek. "You be careful, darlin'. Don't give her any chance to get near ya. She ain't done with you, ya know."

"Yeah, I know, and I ain't got no plans of turnin' my back to her. I love ya, darlin', and I'll be by to check on you sometime in the afternoon. So, until then, you be safe and keep your eyes open. Ya hear me?"

"Yes, darlin', I will. Have I ever told ya, you're pretty cute when you're worried?"

"I'd like to believe ya think I'm cute no matter what is goin' on." Rayne smiled, then gave her a kiss on the lips.

Lisbet pulled away. "If I don't let ya go now, I ain't gonna be lettin' ya go. So out the door, darlin', before I decide to not let ya go at all."

183

With one more slow, soft kiss on the lips, the deputy headed out.

Once outside, Rayne climbed up on her horse and headed towards town. "God help you, Maddie."

†

Rayne brought her running horse to a stop in front of the saloon, jumped down, tethered the horse to a hitching post, and stormed into the bar. The anger she felt was palpable. "Where the hell is that whore?" she shouted, as her heels hit the floorboards hard. The lively music from the piano and the laughter that had filled the room stopped abruptly. "Where is she?" she yelled again.

"Who the hell do you think you are to burst in here and disrupt our good time?" a voice shouted from a corner of the room.

As people's heads turned in the direction the voice came from, Rayne's cold eyes zeroed in on the man who sat with his black hat pulled over his eyes, the glass of beer slowly rising to his mouth.

"Mister, I don't believe we've met before, have we?" Rayne walked towards him.

"Nope, we ain't never met, Deputy." The man took a drink of his beer then put the glass back on the table. "Mind tellin' me what makes ya think ya can call these girls here whores?"

"Cuz they are. And just who the hell are you?"

"It don't much matter who I am. It does matter that you learn some respect for these here women. They cain't help the lot they have."

Rayne's hand rested on the butt of her Colt, ready for anything that might happen, as she slowly approached the table. "I don't much like a stranger tellin' me who I should respect and what not. Ya wanna share your name with me, tell me why you're gracin' our little town?"

"I got word a while back that my brother had been shot dead in a town called Telluride in Colorado. Way I heard it was he was shot in the back by a woman who weren't happy bein' a woman. Can ya imagine that? Guessin' that ya can, considerin' that you're standin' there pretendin' you're a man."

Rayne took a breath. Oh God, this was her nightmare come true. Only in her nightmare, she was standing in the street twenty paces away from a man dead set on killing her, and she could see the bullet leaving the barrel of the gun. She felt it hit square in her chest, and she felt herself hit the ground. She hadn't imagined a conversation about whores and respect.

"Well now, ya heard the story wrong. See, I've only had the misfortune of killin' one man durin' a shootout, after he and a friend of his murdered and robbed a good man. This man, he was a miner, and well, he liked to drink and gamble and run his mouth. I had a feelin' this fella and his friend were up to no good. So, after their card game, I followed them to ol' Horace's place. I got there too late to keep 'em from killin' Horace. They came out and shot at me. I shot back. Hit one fella and the other got away. I'm gonna assume that he was a liar as well as a murderin' coward, since you're here sayin' I shot your brother in the back."

"The man had a name. Henry…his name was Henry," the stranger said, slowly raising narrowed eyes to look at Rayne. "Now ya see, while I don't rightly care what he done,

I do care that he's dead. Henry Wright was my half brother, my baby brother, and ya killed him." The man scooted his chair back, and the people in the room moved away, expecting a gunfight. He stood, reached in his pocket, and pulled out a coin he tossed on the table. "Be seein' ya, Deputy." He walked past Rayne and out into the darkness.

The patrons in the saloon let out a collective sigh. Rayne turned slightly, as she gazed out into the dark night. She took a deep breath, as she walked to the bar and reached for the glass of whiskey Jonas poured for her. Shakily, she brought the glass to her lips and tossed her head back. The liquid burned all the way down her throat. With little thought, she held the glass out for Jonas to pour another, which she drank in one swallow. When she placed the glass on the bar, Jonas filled it once more. She drank it and placed a coin on the bar. She walked out, forgetting all about confronting Maddie. She needed to think.

†

Rayne cautiously walked to the sheriff's office. After being shot at once that evening and having the brother of a man she'd shot and killed in town, she wasn't feeling all too safe. She needed a place to think, a place with one entrance where she could see someone comin'. She sat near the wood stove with the rifle laid across her lap. The more she thought about things, the more she decided that Maddie didn't have reason to want her dead, and wouldn't have troubled herself to find her way in the dark to try to shoot her. Then again, how would a stranger have known where to look for her?

The door opened and Hawks stepped in, his hands going into the air immediately, as Rayne lifted the rifle. "Whoa there, it's just me."

"Sorry, Clinton, I just…"

"Ya wanna tell me why ya got that rifle there ready to blow my head off?" Hawks walked in the rest of the way, taking off his hat and putting it on his desk. "Last I heard you was headed to have supper with your lady and Harry and Etta."

"Yup, had a mighty fine supper too, nice walk as well. Was really enjoyin' it all, right up until someone decided to take a shot at us. I was figurin' it was Maddie all the way in, until I walked into the saloon hollerin' for the whore. Did ya know that fella I shot and killed out at Horace's shack had a brother? The fella's name was Henry. I met his brother tonight. He'd heard that a woman deputy had shot the man in the back. I'm thinkin' he aims to kill me."

"Was he alone?" Clinton opened his desk drawer and pulled out the bottle of whiskey.

"Near as I could tell. He walked out alone, leastwise. Clinton, I done a lot of things in my life that have caused me to be afraid. Things that I ain't proud of. You asked me if I'd ever killed before, and I told ya that I had. I went to Willow Springs when I thought I'd killed my father." Rayne saw Clinton's look of shock. "I just couldn't take one more beatin' from him." She laughed without humor. "Such a fine upstandin' man—a man of God, made his family obey him with his fists." Rayne looked at Hawks, who had been listening quietly. "Lucky me, I hadn't killed the bastard. No, the first one was a man who forced his way into my home. He was of a mind to assault Lisbet. I was faster than him. I shot him dead in self-defense.

187

"After some time and healin', Lisbet and me, we went on with life as a married couple. Built up our ranch, made a home, and was happy. Ben came to live with us, and we was happy.

"Then that son-of-a-bitch of a father of mine showed up at my place, dead set on killin' me. Again, I was faster. The one thing I ain't never done is shoot a man in the back. I ain't never gone looking for trouble. Why's it always seem to find me?"

"Rayne, I've known some bad people, and trust me when I say that you ain't one of 'em. Shit happens to good people that makes 'em bad. You go catch some shuteye in that cell over there. Come first light, we'll pay a visit to this here stranger and see what he has in mind."

With a crooked smile, Rayne replied, "Yup, a little sleep sounds good, but I already know what's on his mind." She stood up and walked to the cot against the cell wall.

Chapter Fifteen

Maddie walked down the stairs to a fairly empty saloon. An occasional table still had a man or two sitting there gambling away the last of his money or passed out with his head lying on the table.

"Mornin' Jane, how was your evenin'?" she asked, all smiles. "Martha got breakfast goin' yet?"

"Where you been? Ya missed all the excitement last night." Jane made her way from the bar to where Maddie stood.

"Jonas gave me the night off, so I took me a little walk. What happened?"

"There's a stranger in town, had some words with the deputy. He seemed nice, I mean he stuck up for us girls. Rayne came here shouting for…uh, well, I think she was lookin' for you."

"Rayne was lookin' for me? I should go to the sheriff's office. I'm…I'll see ya later." she headed towards the doors.

"Ain't ya wanna hear the rest?" Jane asked to the fleeing back.

"Not right now." Maddie kept walking away briskly.

✝

Maddie flew in through the door, all cheerful and smiles. "Howdy, Sheriff, I heard that Rayne was looking for me. Where is she?"

"Where were you last night?" Rayne asked, as she walked out of the cell, buttoning the last button on her shirt.

"Rayne, what are you doin' comin' from that cell?"

Rayne wasn't in the mood for questions coming from the redhead. Her patience was low, her back hurt, and her head was aching. "Maddie, I ain't in the mood. I'm tired, I slept like shit, and someone tried to kill me last night. So one more time…where were ya last night?"

"I…Jonas gave me the night off, so I went out for a walk. Wait. You don't think…you don't think I was the one tryin' to kill ya do ya?"

"Where was ya walkin'? Was it after takin' a ride out on Sutter road, past Harry and Etta's place? Ya know, it was dark, but I could swear I saw a flash of that red hair of yours as ya ducked behind a tree."

"No. Why would I wanna kill you? I love you. Now, that bitch you say is your wife, her I might be tempted to."

Clinton stepped between Rayne and Maddie. "Maddie, I can't decide if ya just don't care about what comes out of your mouth, or if you're just that stupid. But I gotta tell ya, I've watched Rayne turn away from your insults to the woman she loves, and keep ahold of her patience and temper when, honest to God, I don't know that anyone else

190

would have. She's told ya more than once that she ain't interested in pursuin' anything else with ya, and ya just keep tryin'. Now, considerin' that I'm a patient man, and you've done a bit of disruptin' the peace here in my town, well, that and the fact that someone tried to gun down my deputy last night; it's time I put the law down. Let it go with my deputy and her wife, or get outta my town."

Maddie looked from Clinton to Rayne. "I'm sorry, but I don't think you can speak for Rayne. And I sure as hell ain't gonna leave town if I don't want to."

"Here's the thing Maddie, I agree with the sheriff. I don't want you, and I don't know how else to state it so that ya understand."

Maddie's face grew red with anger, but she managed to keep her voice civilized. "Well fine then, I'll be headin' back to the saloon. I'm sorry to have bothered ya so much Deputy." She turned and walked out, leaving both Rayne and Clinton looking at each other.

After a minute or two, Hawks said, "I do believe it's advisable that ya give Maddie some space and stay away from the saloon for a while."

"Yeah, you might be right. Did she just…did that just really happen?" Rayne asked unsure what to think or say.

"I believe for the moment that it did. With very little bloodshed I might add. Though, I wouldn't turn my back on that one just yet. Let's go deal with the matter of the stranger in town." Hawks reached for his hat, and together they walked out of the office towards the hotel.

†

Clinton walked up to the front desk. "Howdy, Lucille. There's a stranger here in town, rode in last night. Rayne, can ya describe him for Lucille?"

"Yup, he was about six foot two, shaggy dark hair, scraggly beard, a lean man." Rayne recalled the man she'd spoken to the night before.

"I know who you're talkin' about. He rode out before sun up. Gave me this to give to ya Deputy." The white-haired woman behind the counter handed Rayne the folded paper. "Told me you'd be by sometime this mornin'."

Rayne looked at the paper that was handed to her. She looked at Hawks, as she tapped the note on the counter. "Thanks." She stepped away from the sheriff, and unfolded the paper.

So, Deputy, I'm imaginin' by now you're right scared. A wonderin' when that bullet is gonna hit ya or from where it's a comin' from. I didn't want it to be like this. Fact is, I wanted to shoot you right where you stood last nite. But then I seen the fear in yur eyes, and I figured this was gonna be a lot more fun. Don't ya agree?

I think I like the idea a you lookin' over yur shoulder. Trust me when I say you're never gonna know when you'll die, but you will.

Until next time, Deputy Mathews
Yours truly
Jacob Jenkins

"Well, he left me a delightful note." Rayne handed Hawks the folded paper. She put her hands on her hips and looked towards the door. She felt like she was never gonna be able to get back to her life with Lisbet. She just couldn't see putting Lisbet and Ben in danger, and she couldn't imagine how she was gonna get Lisbet to understand that. She shook her head and sighed. "I gotta go talk to Lisbet, she needs to take Ben and head back home where she'll be safe."

"Now, wait a minute there, Mathews, shouldn't ya think about this?" Hawks followed her out the door.

Rayne stopped and turn as she stepped out onto the boardwalk. "Nothin' to think about." She faced the man. "I can't have them livin' here when there's lunatics out to kill me. I ain't gonna do that to em'." Rayne began walking again.

"Will you just stop and think for a minute?" Clinton reached out and grabbed Rayne's arm. "Ya can't put your life on hold just a waitin' for someone to shoot ya."

"The hell I can't. It's a lot better than the thought of either Ben or Lisbet bein' killed instead of me. Now, let me go so's I can speak with my wife."

Rayne began walking to the stable where her horse was corralled. She came to a dead stop when Maddie appeared in front of her with a pistol aimed straight at her.

"Whoa, hold on there Maddie."

"You think you can just dismiss me like ya did?"

"Maddie, we can talk about this." Rayne held her hands up in front of her, as she tried to calm the redhead down.

"Ha, when I wanted to talk about us, all you wanted to do was tell me how you didn't wanna be with me. And now ya wanna talk?" Maddie continued, holding the gun in her shaking hands. "You think you're gonna screw me, then walk away? No, I don't believe I'm gonna stand for that."

"Maddie, no. No, I don't think that at all." Rayne took a step forward.

"Stop, don't come any closer, or I'll shoot."

Hawks had headed away from Rayne but turned around, set on talking some sense into his deputy. He spotted Rayne halted in the street, so he quickly stepped against the building and pulled his gun. He carefully made his way closer to his deputy. As he approached the mercantile, he crouched behind the wooden barrels. He had been lucky enough that Maddie was completely engrossed in Rayne and nothing else around her, so he could get safely across from Rayne. With his gun pointed at Maddie, he shouted, "Drop the gun, Maddie, let's talk about all this."

A startled Maddie spun the gun towards the voice that had just shouted at her. "No, there is no talkin' about any of this. If Rayne ain't gonna be with me, then she ain't gonna be with no one," she screamed and pointed the gun back to Rayne. A gunshot shattered the silence of the street.

Chapter Sixteen

The wagon pulled up to the ranch house, and Ben ran to greet Harry as he climbed down and reached for Etta. "Hawwy, Hawwy, I miss you!" He wrapped his arms around the man.

"Hey there, little man." Harry picked the boy up and swung him around. "I've missed you too!" He drew the boy into a hug.

Lisbet walked out the door, wiping her hands on a dishcloth. "Howdy, you two, come in. Dinner is just about ready."

Etta walked up and drew Lisbet into a tight hug. "How are you, hun?"

"I'm doing alright...grateful for the company. I gotta tell ya, I'm goin' crazy with hearin' my own voice. I mean, Ben tries, but there really isn't much companionship an energetic little boy can provide."

"Energetic? Can ya imagine how he'd be if he didn't have all this space to run around in?" Harry walked up to the two, the little boy in his arms giggling as he tickled his ribs.

"Yes, it's a good thing. I honestly can't wait for Rayne to get home. This cattle buyin' trip is takin' way too long." Lisbet smiled at her friends and son.

For Lisbet, the weeks after Maddie's death were a series of ups and downs. The couple had spent most of their days arguing about being a family again, and nights making love. Lisbet would hold Rayne after she woke up from the nightmares in which she dreamt it had been her that had killed Maddie instead of Clinton. Lisbet eventually made a case for reuniting her family, regardless of the dangers, and the family bought the ranch they had fallen in love with. Rayne still served as deputy on a part time basis but was thrilled to finally get back to ranching and watching Ben run and play. And Lisbet…well Lisbet was thrilled to be right where she belonged, in Rayne's home and bed. The place she planned to live the rest of her life.

THE END (maybe)

About the Author

Dannie Marsden

Let me introduce myself. I am Dannie, a butch-identified writer. I am committed to a beautiful woman who is going to become my wife this fall. We have three wonderful children and one adorable granddaughter.

I started writing about ten years ago, and of course, my stories are centered on, what else…beautiful, lesbian women. I try to write about strong women with vulnerabilities and soft caring women who complement, understand, and support them. I hope I convey the many levels women have and the beauty of each level.

Other Books from Affinity eBook Press

Back in the Saddle by Ali Spooner
The crew from *Cowgirl Up* are back in the saddle for more fun. In their new adventure, Coal, Stormy, and Gene get the chance to be part of something they have always dreamed of—a cattle drive. Even without the gang being at the MC2 ranch, there's still plenty of action going on with a new addition, Doc Bo, brings a hint of jealousy and maybe the start of a new romance. Pull on your boots and hats, and hold on tight as you ride along with the crew of the MC2.

Fortunes by Alane Hotchkin
Despite the curves life has thrown Remmy Garrick, her life is going along pretty good except mysterious things keep happening at her job sites. State Investigator Kira Kirpatrick is assigned the case, and everything about Remmy draws Kira to her. Circumstances beyond their control throw their lives into a frenzy. Does Kira have the courage to step up and accept the love Remmy is offering, or will she continue to hide behind her secrets and let them control her?

Captivated by Annette Mori
Juliet Lewis has one too many quirks for her own well-being. Snooping was bound to get her in trouble. Sexy police officer Tanner Sullivan gets Juliet's attention and she wants to know more. Will Tanner turn out to be her jailor or savior? Sparks fly when the obsessive-compulsive Juliet and the paranoid

Tanner cross paths in this quirky thriller with a new twist around every corner.

Pausing by Renee MacKenzie
Jordy Chapman is the Emergency Service Coordinator at Cypress Haven mental health facility in Naples, FL. Keira Yeager's family owns an upscale furniture store in Naples and orchestrates a generous donation of furniture to Cypress Haven. When the two meet, they hit it off immediately. Will a Yeager family's anguish and misunderstanding threaten their new relationship?

Breaking the Silence by JM Dragon
Still grieving five years after the death of her father, Dilana Sterling is a shadow of the woman she once was...a successful author with a string of best sellers, and a longer string of women. Rachael Alderman, a teacher at the local orphanage, lives a quiet, yet satisfying life. When Dilana and Rachael meet, they develop a friendship that leads them on personal journeys of self-discovery. Will their memories of the past prevent them from moving toward each other, or will they find a path that leads to each other so they can experience life together?

The Termination by Annette Mori
Codee is having a bad day and it's only going to get worse. Sawyer, a compassionate young woman, is resigned to her fate. Her only question is what fate is that? After slipping on ice, Codee wonders if she is hallucinating and fallen into an Alice type rabbit hole. The only thing she knows is that she needs to save Sawyer. Enjoy this satirical romance, with all of its twists and turns, that just might make you go hmm...

Dannie Marsden

The Next Time by Erin O'Reilly
What if you had the chance to make history stop repeating itself? Would you sacrifice today for a chance at a better tomorrow. There is a moment in everyone's life that defines their future. For Jac and Carol, that time is now. Jump ahead twenty-five years and meet Carol's granddaughter Livvy. She is ready for a challenge and is fleeing the nest and getting on with her life. Read this wonderful love story that spans several lifetimes.

Open Your Heart a Sensual Collection by Ali Spooner
Excite your senses, rejuvenate your memories and best of all flirt with the edge of eroticism. Allow us to help you relive that first kiss, flirting with young love, your dream come true, surprise encounters, and your wildest desires... Enjoy these stories of love, sweet seduction, and steamy encounters. Open Your Heart...a sensual collection.

Secret of Stone Creek by Natalie London
Jennifer Cameron arrives in Stone Creek, Wisconsin to sell her grandparents' large Victorian home. While there she is intrigued by a twenty-four-year-old never solved murder. Her attraction to the lovely and mysterious librarian, Diana vies for her attention. Follow this suspenseful whodunit to its conclusion.

The Promise by JM Dragon
An accidental meeting with Melissa Grant, leads to an unexpected offer for Kris Lake—refurbishing a beach cottage, with the help of Melissa's granddaughter Claire. Do outer imperfections prevent them from reaching the beauty

that lives inside and the chance of a happy new life? Find out in this lovely romance that will fill you with heart-warming sensations throughout the story.

Christmas at Winterbourne by Jen Silver
The Christmas festivities for the guests booked into Winterbourne House has all the goings-on of a traditional holiday. The only difference is that this guesthouse is run by lesbians, for lesbians. Join the guests and staff at Winterbourne for a Christmas you'll not soon forget.

The Review by Annette Mori
Silver Lining, a successful lesbian romance writer, has the crazy idea to sponsor a contest where the first reader who posts a review wins a home-cooked meal with an offer to fly the winner to Washington State. Jasmine, the winner, has engaged in subtle flirtations with Silver. Bizarre messages from the unknown fan has Silver questioning the wisdom of a relationship with Jasmine.

South of Heaven by Ali Spooner
Kendra Drake has taken over as Captain of her father's shrimp boat. As a favor to her father, Kendra has agreed to give fellow shrimper, Lindsey Bowen, a chance to work on the boat but first must prove herself to Kendra and her crew. Lindsey finds a way into Kendra's heart. Will it only last for the summer?

Catch to Release by Lacey Schmidt
On the verge of success, lesbian folk-rock star, Shay Greenaura, finds herself caught up in more than just her music. Threats have her manager hiring a security firm for

protection. Addison Weller, a former Diplomatic Security Services agent is called in to assess the threats against Shay. Their undeniable attraction, brewing silently between them, could prove to be a fatal distraction. Follow this fast-paced adventure to its surprising romantic conclusion.

Ready for Love by Erin O'Reilly
Kylie Wilcox's life dramatically changed with the death of her husband. Dr. LJ Evans, a renowned archaeologist, needed and wanted nothing but her work for her happiness. Their worlds are about to collide and lives will be altered forever.

Neptune's Ring by Ali Spooner
In the sequel to *Venus Rising*, Nat and Liz, owners of Venus Rising, invite Levi and Vanessa to join them in a venture for a new club on another island. They find the perfect place in an unfinished resort, Neptune's Ring. While on the island, Levi is drawn into a mystery involving secret compartments and a murder. Join the characters in this page-turning adventure, filled with steamy romance, intrigue, and an unsolved murder.

The Ultimate Betrayal by Annette Mori
Lara is a successful, beautiful, charming, financier. She is also a total control freak, so whatever Lara wants, Lara makes sure she gets. Rachel is Lara's fun-loving, charming, irresistible wife. Sophia's surprise visit to see Lara sets in motion a number of life changing events for them all. Hell has no fury as a woman scorned.

Affinity
Rainbow Publications

eBooks, Print, Free eBooks

Visit our website for more publications available online.

www.affinityrainbowpublications.com

Published by Affinity Rainbow Publications
A Division of Affinity eBook Press NZ LTD
Canterbury, New Zealand

Registered Company 2517228